Helping Maisie

By David Hubbard

Chapter 1

'You probably don't remember any of this, do you?'

'No, I think I do. It hasn't been that long.'

'But you've grown up a lot since you last came here.'

'Not according to mum, I haven't.'

Aunt Bella laughed and turned to look at Simon in the backseat.

'You need to eat up, sweetie, that's what you need. I'll sort that out right away when we get in, don't you worry.'

'It's fine, I'm not all that hungry.'

'You're a growing boy, you're always hungry.'

'Honestly, I'm…'

'There's a casserole in the slow cooker. It's your favourite… chocolate chicken.'

'You mean beef?'

'That's not what you called it when you were little.'

A speed bump interrupted Simon's reply. Probably for the best.

He looked out of the window just in time to glimpse something grey and flat between the cliffs stretching off to the horizon.

'You don't get that kind of view in London, do you?'

Simon didn't reply.

'It's too late for a swim now but how about you go down to the beach with us tomorrow? We like to go out before the dog walkers get there.'

'I'd love to but I might be a bit tired from the journey.'

'Oh nonsense! You can get an early night tonight. We'd love the company, wouldn't we Aled?'

Uncle Aled grunted. He didn't shift his hands from the steering wheel.

'See?'

Simon forced a smile. It seemed to satisfy his aunt as she turned round just in time to see the town emerging from between the hills.

'Here we are. Your new home.'

***

It was spitting slightly as Simon got out of the car. One endless cloud filled the sky and dipped into the water at the horizon. Everything looked like it'd had its colour worn away by the sea wind. Even the trees looked grey. Aunt Bella appeared at his shoulder.

'Beautiful, isn't it? Here, you're a big strong lad. You can take the suitcase. Aled's back isn't what it once was.'

But Uncle Aled was already wheeling the case up the cottage path.

'Ah. Well, you can take the fish then.'

'The what, sorry?'

'The fish, sweetie. They're in the boot.'

Sure enough, when Simon opened the boot he was met by two gaping mouths with round dead eyes staring up at him from a puddle on the tarpaulin. They were huge. Aunt Bella poked one of them gently as if to check whether it was still alive.

'Huh, I guess the ice must have melted.'

Simon grimaced.

'Yeah, guess it did.'

He rolled up his sleeves, making a pointed effort to breathe through his mouth.

'I'll just wrap them in the tarpaulin then and…'

'Oh no, don't be squeamish. Just carry them as they are. They won't bite!'

'No, I think I'll just…'

'Your mum was right after all.'

'I'm sorry?'

'You do need a bit of toughening up.'

She tapped him on the shoulder. Simon took in a deep breathe, ready to argue back, but all that came out was a gag at the smell wafting out of the car. Aunt Bella chortled and walked off into the house. Simon stood out by the car for a minute longer then grabbed one fishtail in each hand and followed her.

***

'Oh come on, you can take more food than that.'

'Really, I'm not that hungry.'

'Nonsense! You're wasting away in front of me. Here, have another spoonful at least.'

Aunt Bella snatched the ladle from his hand and poured casserole onto Simon's plate until it lapped at his thumb. She paused for a moment, looking at him expectantly.

'Thank you.'

'You're welcome.'

Simon took a seat at the table and speared a piece of beef on his fork and started chewing. He couldn't deny it tasted pretty good.

'This is delicious. Just like how I remember it.'

'Um, sweetie?'

'I'm sorry?'

Aunt Bella and Uncle Aled were holding each other's hands with their free hands extended across the table to him.

'Oh, right! I'm so sorry.'

Uncle Aled grunted. Aunt Bella smiled. Simon took their hands, suddenly aware of the layer of casserole still on his thumb.

'Lord Jesus. Thank you so much for the blessing of family. It is such a privilege to be able to sit down with our little nephew and feed him once again. I pray that while he's here he will learn what it is to be a man. This evening will be the first of many in his journey into a new life as a mature and responsible adult. I pray that, through us, you will grow him into a strong man of God and that strength starts with food. Bless this meal and bless all of us… especially Simon. Amen.'

'Amen.'

Uncle Aled had spoken for the first time that evening.

'Amen.'

Simon waited a moment before tucking into his meal. As expected, he could feel himself getting full after just a few mouthfuls.

'So Simon.'

Aunt Bella was watching his fork travel from plate to mouth and back.

'What sports do you play?'

'Oh, I don't really.'

'Nothing?'

'No. I mean, I like to run sometimes.'

'Athletics? What distance?'

'Oh, I meant just around the park.'

'Nice. That's nice.'

Aunt Bella smiled.

'Did you hear that, Aled?'

Uncle Aled grunted. His plate was almost empty already.

'What about hobbies? Do you have any of them?'

'I don't know. Um, I like music I guess. Maths too but that's not really a hobby is it?'

'What kind of music? Christian music? Secular?'

'Um, I don't know. Whatever really, a bit of rap.'

'Aha. Rap, okay. Do you play any instruments?'

'Keyboard, a bit. I've been learning the drums too.'

'Nice. Well, no drumming here. We like our sleep! Don't we, Aled?'

Uncle Aled grunted.

'Please, Simon. Keep eating.'

Simon picked up a reluctant forkful. The pile of food on his plate was as tall as ever.

'There's still plenty in the pot so I hope you brought your appetite.'

'Like I said, I'm really not all that hungry.'

'You won't get big and strong if you don't eat up.'

Simon didn't say anything. Each smile was taking more effort than the last.

'After we wash up and you've unpacked, should we start looking for jobs?'

'Jobs?'

'You need to apply soon if you want to find some work.'

'I've only just got here.'

'Exactly, they won't be expecting you.'

'Who won't be expecting me?'

Simon's head was suddenly full of images of him crouching in a bush somewhere with a massive net, ready to jump out at the first employer that drifted past.

'Your mother told me that I need to be firm with you. You can't just sit around here doing nothing like you did at home.'

'I won't.'

'Welsh lads need to go out and earn their own money. Isn't that right, Aled?'

Uncle Aled grunted.

'Yeah, I mean it's the same for us in England.'

'Sure.'

Aunt Bella's smile was almost convincing. Simon set his cutlery down.

'I'll get a job, I will. We can have a look tonight.'

'After we do the washing up.'

'After we do the washing up.'

***

Sure enough – once all of the china plates were sparkling clean and stacked afresh in the cupboard, and the knives and forks were twinkling in the drawer, and Simon's leftovers were festering unforgotten in the compost – Aunt Bella sat down in the middle room and pressed the power button on the computer. It was almost as old as the nephew stood behind her. They watched quietly as the screen scrolled the start-up text. Simon reached into his pocket.

'It might be quicker if we just use my phone?'

'This works too, sweetie. It's just a bit slower.'

'Right.'

A password box appeared on the screen after another moment. Aunt Bella's index finger hesitantly punched in a needlessly long string of letters. The waited silently as the machine pondered whether to let them in or not. Uncle Aled started snoring from his armchair in the room next door.

'Do you have WiFi?'

'What was that, sweetie?'

'WiFi. You know, um, like the internet?'

'Oh yes we have the internet.'

'Right, but wireless. You know?'

'Wireless?'

'You know what? I'll just have a look.'

'Don't unplug anything, please.'

Much to Simon's relief there was a little box under the desk blinking tired green lights at him. He put the password into his phone and stood up to the welcome buzzing of notifications flooding in.

'Here we are.'

Aunt Bella was still transfixed by the screen.

Only two job listings came up for the area which, to be honest, were two more than Simon had expected to see. One was a vague request for a young male cleaner without any contact information. The other was a four year old listing for a cashier job at a souvenir shop.

'Your mother was right to send you here.'

'What do you mean? It'd be a lot easier getting a job back in London.'

'Exactly. It's good to have a challenge.'

Simon's head was starting to ache. The drive across Wales was never fun, nor was the inevitable argument he'd had right before leaving. He pinched the bridge of his nose. Aunt Bella didn't notice.

'Don't you worry, I can help you look. Round here everyone knows everyone. If there's a job to be done we'll find it together.'

'Thanks, Bella.'

'Auntie.'

'Thanks, Auntie. I'm sorry but is it cool if I go up to bed. It's been a long day and I kind of just want to have a bit of sleep.'

'Of course, sweetie. I know what you youngsters are like. There's a towel at the end of your bed and if you need anything I'm just across the hall.'

'Thank you.'

***

Every single room in the house was a different colour. Unfortunately for Simon the guest bedroom was yellow; the shade of yellow they use for the lines along the side of the road. The room was somehow empty and cluttered at the same time. The few available surfaces in the room were hiding under doilies, picture frames and antique lamps. About five Virgin Marys were staring at him and a couple of dozen clones of his cousin Huw waved at him through several layers of sunburn and faded ink at various seaside cafes.

Simon had only brought a single suitcase and rucksack with him. No room for decorations. All he could do was plug his phone on to charge and hang his clothes in the wardrobe. The skinny jeans, oversized jumpers and vintage shirts looked like artefacts from another planet. The Ikea wardrobe may as well have been leading him into Narnia. The thought made him smile for a moment.

His phone buzzed from the desk. Simon changed into pyjamas and threw the dirty clothes onto floor by his suitcase - he'd pick them up in the morning - and climbed into bed. The mattress was only a couple of inches of foam resting on a wooden board. He folded his one pillow in half and propped his head up to look at his phone.

Two missed calls from mum. Five texts from her. He'd read them tomorrow. A handful of nothing emails. Messages from a couple of friends wishing him luck, saying they'd miss him. He skipped past all the other notifications.

A soft knock came at his door. Aunt Bella was trying to be quiet for some reason.

'We'll wake you up for the beach at six.'

'Six?'

'We thought we'd let you have a little lie in.'

Simon looked at the clock and started doing the math on how many hours of peace that gave him.

'Sleep well!'

***

In the dead of night the water turned black. The ocean that had looked so dull and flat to Simon during the day threw itself against the cliffs, desperate to climb up onto dry land. A couple of lonely ships cut through it as the darkness stretched on, each one shining as much nervous light into the void as they dared. By the time the sun peered over the horizon the sea was back to its docile self, snoring softly.

***

'You aren't going to stay in there all day, are you?'

Aunt Bella's voice swam into Simon's dreams far too early and pulled him up, back onto that hard mattress. Simon cracked open one eye just enough to read the time. 5:45.

'I thought you said you'd wake me up at six.'

He heard a chortle through the door and the sound of Aunt Bella trotting off downstairs. Looks like he didn't have any say in this, he had to get up. Back home Simon would have hopped in the shower, done his hair, and picked out an outfit for the day. Instead he just sat on the foot of his bed staring at nothing letting yawn after yawn wash over him, his brain too tired to do anything else.

Footsteps scampered back to his door and there was a knock.

'Wakey, wakey!'

5:47.

'I'm awake, I'm aw…'

Simon had to pause to let out another yawn.

'…ake.'

He pulled on his jeans from the previous night and grabbed the thickest jumper he owned.

***

'Oh no, sweetie.'

'What?'

'You can't wear that.'

'Wait, why not?'

'Let me feel it.'

'What's wrong with it?'

'No, no, no. Not good enough at all!'

'It's the warmest thing I've got.'

'Well you might have to buy some new clothes then.'

'I'll be fine. It's really warm, genuinely.'

'No, you'll freeze out there, won't he Aled?'

Uncle Aled grunted from another room.

'See?'

'I haven't got a warmer jumper to change into.'

'Oh that's okay, you can borrow one of Huw's old ones.'

'Um, are you sure? It's just…'

'Just what, sweetie?'

'Well, I don't think they'd fit me, I guess.'

'Nonsense, he wasn't too much bigger than you.'

Sure enough Aunt Bella did find something. Simon could only imagine the looks on the faces of the sheep if he showed them what their hard-grown wool had gone on to make. Before he could say anything Aunt Bella had smothered his head in it. For a moment the world smelled like the sea breeze, bonfires, and dead fish until Simon found the hole and came up for air. Looking down he saw the jumper was reaching towards his knees and scratching at everything in between. Aunt Bella was beaming at him.

'Perfect.'

Uncle Aled appeared behind him and laughed. Simon couldn't tell whether they were joking or not until suddenly the front door was open and they were leading him out into the morning air in that outfit.

The world couldn't have looked more different from the night before if a bomb had hit it. The grey cloud that had shrouded everything the night before was gone. The few remaining wisps of it smouldered overhead in the morning glow as if the sun had burned all of the drabness away from the world. The little town was so quiet that Simon could hear the sea still yawning by the shore.

'Now do you see why we get up early?'

Aunt Bella squeezed his arm and led him off down the road. The coastline consisted almost entirely of slate cliffs, stabbing up out of the ground like meteorites that had come from the coldest reaches of space. Nestled in between the cliffs were beaches, tiny paradises hidden between the rocks, only visible when the tides were out. In the middle of a storm you'd never know they were even there.

And somewhere, tucked away in a tiny little estuary between two cliffs sat their town. There was one road winding along next to the river right down to the sea before jumping over a bridge and scrambling up the cliff at the last minute. There was one pub, one church, one beach and a dozen or so boats tipped forlornly sideways in the almost empty river bed. A sign outside the pub read *Fresh Crab, The Best in Wales*. Within a couple of minutes of walking Simon had seen the whole town. It was smaller than he remembered.

'Everything we need is right here.'

Aunt Bella's attempt at reading his thoughts had failed spectacularly.

'Sure.'

Simon had to lift about half a foot of jumper to reach into his pockets.

'You've got alcohol, Jesus, and the sea. What else is there?'

Uncle Aled chuckled. Simon couldn't help but grin.

'Where do you buy your food though? I haven't seen a supermarket around at all.'

'We have to go to the city for that.'

'The city?'

'The next town along. It has two and a half thousand people, you know?'

'Does it really?'

'We could never live there though, could we Aled? Too crowded.'

Uncle Aled grunted.

***

The beach wasn't part of the town. It was in the next cove along, heading away from the 'city' along the coastal path. The morning air felt good in Simon's lungs as he climbed the path up the cliff. He only got to enjoy the view out over the ocean for a second before they started down the other side of the hill towards the pebbles that marked the water's edge.

When he was little Simon had used to always climb on this giant rock by the cliff and jump off into the water. Since then the rock had gotten smaller. In fact the whole beach had gotten smaller. What once seemed like an endless cove of shingles, stretching out to the cliffs far in the distance, now just looked like a pokey little pebble beach between two hills. The crashing waves had been replaced by gently lapping sea foam. A trapped crisp packet was inches away from being swallowed up by the water.

'It should be quite warm today.'

Aunt Bella appeared at his shoulder and lifted her jumper over her head.

'Are you excited?'

'I didn't bring my trunks.'

'Well that was silly.'

'Yeah, sorry. I…'

'It's fine, sweetie. We can pop back and get them. It's not far.'

'No, honestly it's fine. You two go in without me.'

'Are you sure? It looks lovely today.'

'I don't really like the sea all that much.'

He shouldn't have said that last bit. Aunt Bella was looking at him. After a moment she shrugged it off and continued stripping her clothes off. Simon just had to stand there awkwardly as his aunt and uncle undressed on either side of him. Fortunately they'd had the foresight to put their costumes on under their clothes. He wasn't sure he'd have been all that comfortable seeing his retired relatives naked at 6:15 in the morning.

Aunt Bella gave one last half-hearted attempt to convince him to go in with them, dancing around the suggestion of skinny dipping, before Uncle Aled took her hand and led her into the water. The waves jumped up at their ankles like a puppy welcoming its owners home. Simon sat down on the pebbles and wiggled around until they made a firm seat under him.

As much as it pained him to admit, Aunt Bella had been right: even in this jumper he could feel the wind squeezing its way between the threads. There wouldn't be any point doing his hair living here either, the wind would turn it into a tangled mop no matter how much hairspray he used.

Simon found a small loose thread on the sleeve and started fiddling with it absently. A cargo ship poked its nose out from behind the cliff face to his right. Simon watched as it crawled along, halfway between himself and the horizon. After a couple of minutes it got to his aunt and uncle. Simon watched them. They weren't playing in the sea, or swimming, or going out far. They just stood there in waist-deep water holding hands, gently bobbing up and down in time with the ocean.

The ship continued on past them along the beach. It was only once it was about to disappear behind the cliff all the way on the other side that Simon spotted a figure stood there at the opposite end of the beach to himself. It was a girl, in an ugly knitted jumper, not too different to the one he was wearing. Her hair was knotted, spilling out over her shoulder, whipping this way and that in the wind.

She was skimming stones into the sea. Throwing them hard, so hard that most of them were going straight under without bouncing once. She was too far away for Simon to see her face. Besides her hair was doing a good job of keeping it hidden. The girl looked like she'd never so much as seen a hairbrush.

Then suddenly she was looking right at him. She straightened up and her head snapped round in his direction. Simon couldn't help but think of a dog when it catches a scent on the wind. Simon raised a tentative hand. This could be the only girl his age, the only person his age, for miles around, even if she did look a bit... alternative.

The girl looked at his wave for a moment before spinning on her heel. She stormed off the beach and up the footpath heading away from town, kicking up stones and dust with every step. Just as she reached the top of the cliff she shot a middle finger back in his direction. Then she was gone before he'd even realised what had happened.

'Don't worry about her.'

Aunt Bella had somehow made it all the way over to him without making a sound. Both she and Uncle Aled glowered in the girl's direction.

'She's...'

But no one filled in the blank for her.

***

They went straight home after that. The wind cut through Simon's jumper as he walked. Uncle Aled and Aunt Bella were talking about something up ahead but Simon wasn't really listening. The tide was coming in, water was tickling the boats still lying there in the estuary. Simon couldn't think of where the nearest boat to his house back in London would even be. In fact he couldn't remember ever setting foot on a sailboat.

From up on the coastal path the town looked like a playset. Like the one Simon used to have as a kid with train tracks running all through his house with intricately modelled fields, trees, and cottages dotted all around it. Looking at the town he couldn't imagine anything exciting ever happening to it. It might not have changed for the last hundred years.

How long would it be until he saw his bedroom again? A couple of months? A year? He wasn't sure how long it would take for him to prove himself to his mum. Since leaving school Simon had been happy to just enjoy a bit of well-earned peace, an extended summer holiday if you would. He'd worked damn hard at school and come out of it with a solid set of grades. That meant he could have some time off, right?

Not according to mum it didn't. He'd only been enjoying his peace for a month maybe – actually, maybe two – when she'd snapped at him. Actually, it might have been three. Didn't make a whole lot of sense sending him out here though. Looking down on the town Simon could see a grand total of two places that could employ him. Neither of them was open.

You can come home when you've proven yourself.

What does that even mean?

It means you can come home when you understand why I'm kicking you out.

Simon understood it alright. She'd forgotten.

She'd forgotten what it was like at school. Working 8:30 to 4:00, to 5:00 for Simon. He wasn't one of those kids who'd mess around during lunch and stare at his phone in lessons, he'd actually worked. Every break time he got, almost every break time he got, he was studying. But no. Apparently he was lazy because he'd come home tired and want to play video games and go on his phone. It just wasn't fair.

Simon checked his phone. No signal. As expected. No messages either. That would've been a long shot though, it was still stupidly early in the morning.

'Are you taking a picture?'

Aunt Bella was smiling up at him from further down the path.

'Uh, yeah. Sure.'

He took a photo of nothing in particular and followed them down the hill back into town.

***

Even though Simon had known how little there was to do before coming to Wales, he was still shocked at just how bored he got. Aunt Bella had to run out to do an errand leaving him and Uncle Aled alone in the lounge, sitting on chairs that were so frilly and chintzy that it was difficult to find any kind of comfort. Neither of them spoke for a long time. Simon busied himself on his phone while Uncle Aled chewed whatever was in his mouth.

After maybe a couple of hours of this Uncle Aled got up and changed into a pair of stained overalls. He looked like a martian stood in front of the china plate collection in the cabinet.

'Car.'

Exhausted from speaking so much Uncle Aled fetched a tool kit from under the stairs and went outside leaving Simon alone in the house for the first time. In most houses this would be an excuse to go exploring, to have a peak in all the rooms he was told not to go in, to properly look at everyone in the pictures, to grab a cookie from the kitchen. Now that he thought about it, Simon wasn't sure if a cookie had ever entered the confines of these walls. Nothing about this house made him want to see more, nothing in this town had piqued his curiosity.

Well, almost nothing.

There must be something up with that girl. She'd been wearing a jumper so ugly it'd made Simon forget his own monstrosity, her hair looked like it had been braided by a hedge, and she'd stuck up her middle finger in this town of all places. That must be illegal here, right? You'd give poor Doris another episode if she saw that.

His phone buzzed. It was mum. He sat for a moment waiting to type out his reply but no words came.

Another message popped up.

Call me?

Simon hit dial before he wimped out. She picked up on the second ring.

'Hey, honey.'

'Hi, mum.'

They both waited for a few seconds.

'How's it going?'

'How are you?'

Simon laughed. There was another pause, longer this time.

'Honey, I'm sorry for shouting at you yesterday.'

'I'm sorry too.'

'This will do you good. I just want what's best for you.'

'I know.'

'You know it'll do you good?'

'I know you want what's best for me.'

'Well, that's a start. How's Bella?'

'She's… still Aunt Bella.'

'Driving you up the wall a bit?'

'Little bit.'

'Get a job then you don't have to be under her rule so much.'

'Yeah I'm working on it. She had me looking at vacancies at like midnight last night.'

'Why does that not surprise me? How's Aled?'

'Fixing the car.'

'I wouldn't expect anything else from that man. How many words has he said to you so far?'

'I think about six?'

'He's really taken a shining to you then.'

'I managed to make him laugh this morning so I think I must be up for some kind of local award.'

'I did always love Aled. There's a heart of gold in that man.'

They lapsed into silence. The hostility that had plagued Simon's departure was gone. At the end of the day, she was still his mum. Sending him here was just her weird way of trying to teach him something.

'You do know it would've been much easier for me to get a job in London? I think there are a grand total of ten people on the welsh coast that aren't retired.'

'It's not just about getting a job, honey.'

'Well, what is it then? What do I have to do to prove that I'm an adult?'

'I don't know yet.'

'Gee, thanks mum.'

'I'm being serious. I've been an adult for years and I still don't really know what it's all about.'

'You know, most parents when they want to teach their kid a lesson will actually have the lesson in mind. They'll make them mow the lawn, or clear out the gutters, not ship them off to another country.'

'Wales hardly counts as another country.'

'I thought children were supposed to be the best thing that happens in your life.'

'Oh they're top five, for sure.'

'Funny.'

'Listen, honey. I've got to dash. You be good.'

'No playing with matches, no talking to strangers, blah blah blah.'

'All that jazz.'

'Love you mum.'

'Love you too.'

Simon took the phone away from his ear to hang up, just before he pressed the button he heard a tiny voice shouting at him.

'And get a job!'

***

The weight had lifted. Simon hadn't even really noticed it was there until it was gone. This had been the first time he'd fought with his mum in what must have been years. Aunt Bella would be back before long. Simon half expected her to walk through the front door, job contract in hand, telling him just how lucky he was to have such a loving aunt.

He'd get a job. He would. He just wished everyone would stop pestering him about it.

Sure enough, it was the first thing out of Aunt Bella's mouth when she got back.

'I saw the vicar just outside and he said the graveyard needs a bit of work.'

'Oh, right?'

'He can't pay you though.'

'Right.'

'And it'd only be about a day's work. The graveyard isn't very big.'

'Okay.'

'Not since half of it fell in the sea.'

'Wait, did it really?'

'Yeah, it wasn't very nice. There was… debris on the beach.'

'Is it safe?'

'The graveyard? Oh, yes. As safe as any coastal path round here.'

'Good to know.'

'I'll keep asking around. You should do this job for him though.'

'Alright, I'm happy to give it a go, I guess. Thanks. I was thinking, would the pub have anything going?'

'I wouldn't know.'

'I might go have a look.'

'Or maybe you couldn't?'

'Why? Is the owner a… uh, not nice?'

Aunt Bella was picking at her sleeve, not quite facing him. When she spoke it was in an uncharacteristically little voice.

'It's just not a good place for a boy like you.'

His mother had mentioned something about teetotalling. Simon made a note to himself not to push that line of enquiry too much. He broke the silence.

'What's the plan for the rest of the weekend then?'

'Well tonight we need to watch the TV. Have you seen *Larkrise to Candleford*?'

'Can't say that I have, no.'

'Well we have all the DVDs and we watch one episode every weekend.'

'Alright.'

'Then we watch the news before bed.'

'Okay cool. I might just pop to bed and get an early…'

'Nonsense. You're family. And families spend time together.'

'Sure.'

If Simon sat at the end of the sofa he reckoned he could be on his phone while they watched without it being too obvious.

***

In the chintzy sitting room, tucked away from the sea wind by stone walls older than the beach from their morning trip, Simon, Aunt Bella and Uncle Aled watched the TV. Little model people in their little model house in the little model town. There wasn't a sound anywhere. Not the sloshing of waves, or the chatter of the television, or the cars on the road. They were all toys. Toys in a room with the lights switched off. All silent. All happy. Except maybe Simon. His phone kept buzzing.

Chapter 2

'Wakey-wakey.'

The darkness broke.

Aunt Bella's voice was at his door.

'We have church in twenty minutes.'

'Got it.'

Simon didn't sound nearly as awake as he wanted. Rolling out of bed he grabbed a bundle of clothes from the wardrobe and the slightly damp towel. There were no notifications on his phone. Not even spam.

'Got it.'

Simon was trying to convince himself more than anyone else.

***

Church was packed. Not because loads of people turned up but because there was only capacity for about fifteen people. Simon, Aunt Bella, and Uncle Aled accounted for a fifth of the congregation alone. By the church's standards his aunt and uncle were spring chickens. He couldn't imagine how alien he must have looked, still submerged in that awful jumper that he'd had to wear again.

Church back home, that had been another story. Over fifty people Simon's age alone. Hundreds in total. Every Sunday there'd be a massive countdown on the screen with thumping dance music behind it. The band would have six members on a quiet week. The whole building would pound with energy.

He couldn't think of anything more different than this tiny stone box of a building. He'd got a splinter from the pew as soon as he sat down. Not that he'd been able to sit down for long. Aunt Bella had paraded him around to every retiree in town as if he was her prized squash. They would all talk about him to Aunt Bella, pointing out how skinny he was, asking about the jumper, and generally commenting on his appearance as if he wasn't there.

With every eye staring at him, Simon went to sit on the back row by the doors. He didn't want to feel the wrinkled faces peering at him over inch thick specs all the way through the service. Aunt Bella saw him sat there and her brow furrowed. She was just about to come over and say something when the vicar took up position behind the lectern and gave something halfway between a death rattle and cough.

Much to his embarrassment, Simon got a special welcome from the front. Apparently it was always nice to see a fresh face on a Sunday morning and who knows, maybe he'll end up clearing up the graveyard. This was met with a dry pattering of applause and several necks craned in his direction. Simon's attempt at a smile felt like more of a grimace. So much for subtlety.

The church was too small to fit an organ, of course. Not that Simon was particularly excited to go back to the hymns of old. Instead someone had plugged a Casio keyboard into a set of grey computer speakers from the early-2000s. A doddery old lady hobbled around to it and smiled right at Simon before playing the first chord. He couldn't remember whether he'd been introduced to her or not.

He was still staring at her trying to remember when someone punched him in the ribs.

'Motherf-'

Simon was lucky everyone in here was at least half-deaf. He turned to see an angry tangle of hair in a God-awful jumper glaring back at him. It was her. From the beach.

'Move.'

Simon was too confused for a moment to know what she meant.

'Oh. Am I in your seat?'

She scrunched up her lips and nodded quickly, not breaking eye contact. Up close her face looked tough, tougher than his.

'Sorry. I'm really sorry.'

He edged sideways and gave her enough space to stand between him and the door. After an overly dramatic sigh, she took it. She was a couple of inches shorter than him and about as skinny. For some reason though, Simon was dead certain she could take him in a fight.

He looked back down at his hymn book and tried to catch where they were in the song. The girl wasn't singing at all. Out of the corner of his eye he could see her head was still angled slightly in his direction.

She didn't have a hymn book. Of course. She couldn't sing along because she didn't know the words. He was just about to offer to share his with her when all of a sudden she joined in at the start of the next verse.

In all of his life Simon had never heard a hymn that sounded good. Especially with an organ. They were about as lifeless as mind numbing as music could possibly get. That was, until that Sunday morning in a tiny grey box of a church by the sea in the middle of nowhere, Wales. Out of the mouth of that girl next to him came a sound that Simon had never heard before. He had no thoughts left in his head. Her voice was, quite simply, the most beautiful thing he'd ever heard. He didn't open his mouth to join in. He just listened.

Simon listened to her sing for all four hymns. They were songs he'd never heard before and when they ended he felt a weird pang in his chest.

The girl sat down on the pew with a huff. It creaked under her. The moment was over. Annoying noises returned to the world. Simon accidentally brushed against her arm as he took his seat beside her. She stiffened but kept her eyes forward. She was biting her lip, hard.

***

The rest of the service went by without much fanfare. Simon had often struggled to keep track of sermons at home where they'd been delivered by plaid shirted twenty-somethings and were all about the Bible's role in social media. Keeping track here would be nothing short of a miracle.

Simon's mind was instead taken up by the girl next to him. She was bouncing her leg constantly. It shook the pew just enough to make a small squeaking sound. It reminded him of the noise old school cartoons would have when a character rubbed their eyes in disbelief. It took all of his restraint not to reach out and grab her leg to hold it still. If he did he wouldn't have been surprised if he'd ended up bouncing up and down too.

What was *she* doing here?

Every time the question bubbled up in his mind Simon tried to push it down. The church is for everyone. There isn't a Christian 'type'. Everyone is welcome. But still. Her? Not that she wasn't welcome. Just, why was she here? She didn't seem like the type. Not that there was a type. What had Aunt Bella said yesterday?

Don't worry about her. She's...

Simon had to admit, he was struggling to come up with a word for her too. Weird?

Everyone is welcome. There isn't a 'type'.

When they all stood to sing one final hymn Simon remained quiet again. When she was singing it was almost possible to forget that he already didn't like her. She glanced his way a couple of times but Simon just kept his eyes fixed forwards, watching the little old lady hunched over her Casio.

They sat down. They vicar wheezed a thank you to everyone for coming. His eyes caught awkwardly on Simon and the girl at the back as he said it. With only a momentary stutter he kept talking, only there was a new note in his voice. He sounded a bit strained.

'Why are you here?'

A small voice spoke next to him. Simon turned to see her glaring at him once more. She had a northern accent, one of the annoying ones.

'I'm here with my Aunt and Uncle. They're letting me stay at theirs for a...'

'No. Why are you *here*?'

She waved a sleeve around the church.

'Oh. Um... I'm a Christian? Always have been.'

'Don't seem like it.'

'Excuse me?'

'Weren't singing, were you?'

'I was...'

Simon caught himself before he told the truth. Might be a bit weird telling her he was listening to her the whole time.

'You what?'

'I was um... I didn't know the words.'

She raised her eyebrows at the hymn book still on Simon's lap. His face felt hot. She was getting up to leave.

'If you don't want to be here then don't be here.'

'I do want to be here.'

'Alright then, what were the three main points in the talk?'

'What's your problem?'

'What book in the Bible was the passage from?'

'What have I done to piss you off?'

'Don't be here if you don't want to be here.'

'That's not a very Christian thing to say. I thought everyone's welcome.'

'Grow a pair and stand up for your beliefs. If you're Christian, live like it. Actually sing along next time.'

Simon bristled. Who the hell did she think she was? He stood and was just raising a finger to shove in her face when he became aware just how quiet the church was. Every pair of eyes was on him. The fight left him like air from an untied balloon. Aunt Bella's voice, too cheerful, rang out.

'Simon, over here! Mabel says her son is looking for lads to work for him.'

He dropped his finger and forced a smile. No one bought it. The girl refused to move out of his way so he had to flatten himself against the pew in front and sidle past her. Conversations started to pick back up around the room.

'You want a job?'

Simon had already passed her when she spoke.

'What?'

'You want a job?'

She was looking at the floor almost halfway between them.

'Yeah. Why?'

'Supermarket's hiring.'

And with that she turned on her heel and walked out to be swept away by the sea wind back up her coastal path.

The whole time that Simon was talking to Mabel - who, as it turned out, did not have a son at all - he kept playing the argument over and over in his mind.

***

The walk home was subdued. For once, Aunt Bella wasn't saying much. After a minute of silence Simon pulled his phone out and started scrolling through nothing in particular. Uncle Aled almost said something but thought better of it.

It had been a weird morning for everyone involved.

After the girl had stormed out Simon proceeded to have just about everyone in the church come up to him. They all effectively said the same thing, in a very indirect, polite way. They didn't blame him for getting annoyed at all. That girl was…

But none of them ever quite finished their thoughts.

'What's her name?'

Simon's question seemed to echo all through the empty street. Aunt Bella, walking ahead of him looked around as casually as she could. She committed to a half-shrug and bobbed her head around a bit.

They walked in silence all the way to the cottage. The paint by the door was chipped. A flake blew off in the wind. Aunt Bella took her shoes off and gave Simon a warm smile before disappearing inside. Uncle Aled made no move to follow her. He looked right at Simon and spoke.

'Maisie.'

Simon felt his aunt tense up on the other side of the door without even seeing her.

'She's… Maisie.'

And without another word they walked into the cottage and closed the door behind them, leaving the wind all on its own in the front garden.

Chapter 3

Everything was still.

The grey clouds heaved their final showers and faded away. The winds that tore at the oceans, throwing walls of water against the cliff, ran out of breath and collapsed on the grassy cliffs and lay there.

The ocean was dozing. It glowed blue. Diamonds of sunlight skimmed across the surface as the sun watched the world nap. Brilliant white clouds filled the sky like palaces. And none of them paid any attention to the tiny little figure eating a sandwich staring up at them.

The grass tickled Simon's bare feet. The world stretched out in front of him. A white painted stone wall, bright as the clouds, jutted out from the grass somewhere off to his right. The wall ran all the way to the edge of the cliff and fell off. Hidden behind it was an equally white chapel the size of a tool shed. Small grey stones stuck up out of the grass around it, each with a name written on it. Many of them had been worn smooth by the wind.

His phone buzzed.

Simon told himself not to check it. After a minute he pulled it out of his pocket anyway. He was surprised he got signal out here. The graveyard sat there patiently waiting for him to come back.

It was Friday. Five days since Simon went to church with his aunt and uncle.

The weather for much of the week had been drab. Just enough rain in the air to leave your skin feeling raw. Simon had planned to stay inside as much as possible but Aunt Bella had other ideas. On Monday she'd taken him to bingo. Actual bingo. Simon had laughed when she first suggested it until he realised that she was being deadly serious.

It had been in the town hall of the neighbouring town. Simon had been introduced to about forty variations of the same old lady, all of whom hugged him and told him he'd need to put on a bit more fat if he was going to make it out here. They each were given a different coloured stamp to use on their little cards. Simon's was a pink cat face that grinned at him every time he won a number. Much to his horror he suddenly had a complete row.

Subtly as he could, Simon tried to lay his arm across the sheet of paper to hide his five Cheshire Cats but Aunt Bella was too fast. Whipping the card into the air she cried bingo loud enough even for Marie with her hearing aids to hear. Silly as it was, Simon couldn't help but feel a little proud of himself as he was handed a smiley face notepad and green pencil for his achievement. In the car home Aunt Bella had gushed about how it had taken her three weeks to get her first bingo.

Every day that week that he'd put off speaking to the vicar about the graveyard Aunt Bella upped her game. On Tuesday, she'd taken him along to her Yoga class. In the car Simon wondered where the nearest gym could possibly be until suddenly they turned off the road into a muddy field with the gate swung wide open. In the middle of the field, dressed in raincoats and wellie boots, stood a gaggle of nine or ten elderly looking ladies huddled like penguins against the never ending drizzle.

'Why are we stopping here?'

Aunt Bella laughed his question off and hopped out of the car. Sure enough, ten minutes later Simon was up to his ankles in mud in his trainers trying to do a downwards dog while a woman four times his age stared at him from between his open legs. She'd winked. Multiple times.

On Wednesday Simon caved and went to see the vicar about the graveyard. He'd rather risk being flushed away into the sea with a tide of dead bodies than go another yoga session with a group of them. No matter how innocent Aunt Bella seemed he was certain that that had been the plan all along. To be fair to her, it had worked.

Simon brushed the crumbs off his legs and got up. It was crazy how the weather can turn around just like that.

All the way up to the graveyard the vicar had talked to Simon in that same gentle wheeze in which he'd delivered his sermon. It was a wonder he managed to make it up the coastal path. The whole time Simon had been waiting for him to exhale slightly too hard. His lungs must have looked like a helium balloon two weeks after a party.

Nevertheless, the old man had made it up to the field where Simon was now putting his shoes back on. It had been raining. There were of course no proper tools to use except one of those old lawn mowers that's literally just a five blades that roll along when you push them. All of which were more rust than metal. Before leaving the old man had handed him a pair of scissors too. The implication there was pretty clear.

Simon barely made a dent on Thursday. The grass springing up around the graves – as Aunt Bella had told him proudly – was Welsh grass. Much tougher than that grass you keep in London. Plus the mower was useless. Plus it was raining. Simon didn't have much choice other than to crawl around on his hands and knees in the rain cutting the grass by hand with kitchen scissors. And the best thing? He wasn't getting a penny for it.

But today – as Simon hopped over the brilliant white wall and landed about six feet above a skeleton – he felt good. The skies had cleared. The wind had exhausted itself and, most importantly, the grass had dried meaning the lawn mower was now marginally more effective than the scissors.

It squeaked as Simon wheeled it around between the headstones and over to the edge of the cliff. Where the fourth wall had once stood there was now a sheer drop into the waters below with only a shred of CAUTION tape fluttering gently between him and the abyss. If he wasn't careful he'd accidentally end up trimming the waves.

Simon paused at the edge, looking out into the water. The slumped headstone to his right was the newest one here. The first to fall the next time the sea felt hungry. It was leaning towards Simon seeking comfort. Or maybe it was comforting him. *I'm a good swimmer, Simon. Don't worry about me.*

Simon patted the stone. It was warm.

Here lies Huw Davies. He made a mean cup of tea. And he was a good lad too. 1985 – 2012.

With a little smile Simon wheeled the mower around and squeaked his way back up between the headstones. The wind perked up its ears at the sound.

***

A cup of tea was waiting for Simon when he got in.

Uncle Aled was still out fishing. Simon had asked if he could join him out in the boat one day but his uncle had just laughed and said 'Get a job.'

Aunt Bella smiled from across the kitchen table as Simon kicked off his shoes.

'How was it?'

'Better. A lot better than yesterday. The grass dried out a bit so I could actually kind of mow it.'

'I made you some tea.'

'Thank you so much.'

He joined her at the table.

'Still no jobs?'

'Still no jobs.'

Simon took a sip then placed his mug down carefully before asking the question.

'What about the supermarket?'

'Huh. That's a good question.'

'I heard they were looking for someone.'

'I don't know anybody who works there. Who told you?'

Aunt Bella was sharp as ever.

'Oh um, I can't really remember.'

'When did you see them?'

'It was um, just a walker I think. Today. Up by the graveyard.'

There was absolutely no way in hell Aunt Bella believed his lie but she let it slide.

'The supermarket. I could drive you there now to speak to them?'

'No, no. Don't worry. I'll see them by myself.'

His aunt looked a little hurt at that.

'It's just that, you know, I'm all covered in mud and sweat from being up the hill all day. First impressions are key.'

Now she was smiling again.

'Of course.'

It was a while before she spoke.

'It's good to see you taking some responsibility.'

Simon took another sip of his tea. He wasn't sure whether that was supposed to be a compliment or not.

***

Somewhere out in the water Uncle Aled stood at the bow of his boat. The sea gently rocked him left to right. Left to right. He gazed up at the cliffs, just about able to see the headstones poking over the edge. He gave a small nod before setting a course for the harbour.

***

The town was silent. Until it wasn't.

The door to the pub banged open spilling noise and light all over the sleeping street. Out stumbled a man, leering at anything that moved. He had a tangle of messy hair tied up out of his eyes.

His pockets were empty. The fruit machines were full.

He balled his fists and staggered up the coastal path.

There'd be money at home.

There better be...

The smell of tea bags swirled around Simon. Then the church broke and fell into the sea pulling him down with it into the cold swirling brew beneath.

'Wakey wakey.'

The dream shrank back into the darkness. Simon felt it glaring at him from the unlit corners in his room.

'What time is it?'

'Time to go to the beach, sweetie. Don't forget your costume this time.'

It was still dark outside.

Simon grabbed at the phone on his bedside table but missed. There was a bang as it hit the floor.

Groaning, Simon rolled over and peered over the edge of his bed. The phone was lying face down on the floor. He flipped it over and saw his face reflected a hundred times in the shattered glass.

It didn't turn on.

'Fuck.'

'What was that, sweetie?'

***

The sea clamped hold of Simon's legs. All of the life rushed out of them immediately. Only the pain and the cold remained.

Aunt Bella and Uncle Aled were already up to their waists ahead of him, holding hands and bobbing up and down.

Simon's lungs refused to breathe properly. The sea wind clawed at his pale chest. The retreating waves pulled him out further.

Somewhere up on the coastal path a tangle of angry hair in an ugly jumper peered up over the cliff top, just far enough to count the three figures out in the water before huffing and turning to go back the way it came.

Simon was too busy thinking about his phone to notice. A weird panic was settling over him. What if there was an emergency? What if Aunt Bella and Uncle Aled were swept off into the sea and he had to call the coastguard? What if someone was taken ill at home? What if he was out alone and broke his leg?

What would he do to keep himself busy?

Read a book?

Aunt Bella was trying to hide her laughter.

He really didn't see the funny side.

At least the cold had woken him up if nothing else.

***

The vicar was thrilled to see Simon at church the next day. He ambled over as soon as caught sight of him and wheezed a dry shower of compliments until he started to sway on his feet. When they went to sit down Simon noticed Aunt Bella scarcely hiding an enormous smile. He couldn't tell if she was feeling smug about his phone or was genuinely pleased with him. It was nice to have her off his back though, even if it was just for a moment.

The Casio droned into life for the first hymn. From somewhere near the back of the church Simon heard that same voice he'd spent all of last week listening to. It cut clearly over the rest of the noise. Simon scowled. He wanted to be defiant to her but he wasn't sure whether that meant singing louder or not singing at all. Of course, he settled on his go-to: sing just loudly enough to hear it yourself.

He refused to look to the back of the hall as they took their seats again.

In fact he was so focused on not looking that he didn't hear his name being called out from the front until Aunt Bella jabbed him in the ribs. The vicar was beaming right at him.

'Simon, my boy. Why don't you come up to the front?'

'Oh.'

Simon banged his knees against the pew in front as he stood. Someone tittered.

Every eye in the building was fixed on him except for one pair right at the back. He glanced at her and kicked himself for it.

His right pocket felt empty without a phone to fill it. The vicar waited patiently for Simon to join him.

Simon wiped his hands against the back of his jeans. It was far too cold to be sweating this much.

'Young Simon here has been a blessing this week.'

Simon shifted his weight back and forth. A pair of eyes glanced at him from the back and looked away quickly.

'The graveyard along the path hasn't been very well cared for since... well, since the incident. This week, however, Simon has stepped in and worked very hard cutting the grass and making it a bit more presentable.'

Simon went to sit down but a wisened hand clasped his elbow with surprising speed.

'As a token of our thanks I thought it best that we get him a present for his hard work.'

Money? A new phone?

'I asked a few of the senior members of the church to chip in.'

All but two of the people in this building could be considered senior members.

'And we bought you these to say thank you.'

It wasn't quite the big reveal anyone had expected. The vicar had to hobble over to the lectern, plant a hand on top and slowly bend down to grab something off the floor. His back clicked four times as he straightened up. He turned back to Simon with a warm smile and held out a plastic bag. It was difficult to see where the wrinkles of his skin ended and those of the bag began. Simon took it and peered inside.

Two black boxes with antennas poking out of the tops. Walkie-talkies.

Simon opened his mouth but the vicar was again too fast for him.

'We weren't quite sure what you kids are into. But then we heard from Bella about your smartphone. And we all know what you kids are like with your technology. Must feel like you've lost a part of you.'

The entire congregation - bar one at the back - nodded gravely in agreement.

'We thought that, with these, you can still talk to all of your friends.'

A pang of loneliness hit Simon. Who could he possibly give a walkie-talkie to? The thought crossed his mind of mailing one back to London and testing the range.

He smiled and thanked the vicar. He hoped it was convincing. It genuinely was quite a sweet present, especially because he could feel the love behind it. They were trying their best to make him feel at home. They really were.

The loneliness subsided as the service went on. Sure he was the only person his age here. Almost the only person. But that wasn't so bad. He could get used to it. Besides, if he got this job at the supermarket maybe he wouldn't have to be here long after all. Before he knew it the service was over. See? Time really was starting to move a bit faster.

Simon glanced towards the back row of the church as he got up from his seat. Maisie was looking at the ground. Even with her face half-concealed by shadow, he could make out a shining black eye. She brushed a lock of curly hair in front of it and slipped out through the narrow gap in the doors.

***

Simon lay awake in bed that night staring up at the ceiling. This was weird.

No matter how long he lay there his brain just wouldn't stop thinking.

When he had his phone with him he could just watch or listen to something until he drifted off.

Now he was just trapped in the silence of the room.

Nothing to distract him from his own thoughts.

Nothing to trick him into falling asleep.

In a few hours he would have to get up.

He wasn't entirely sure where the supermarket was but that was fine, he could just pull up the maps on his phone.

Or not.

He'd find it.

Aunt Bella had said it was about an hour's walk but she'd offered him her bike instead.

He'd declined.

Out in the street a drunk was singing.

It reminded Simon of London in a weird sort of way.

Glass smashed.

Singing turned to shouting.

Simon closed his eyes and fell asleep.

Chapter 4

It was a weird feeling, walking without music.

It was just a staple of modern life. If you're traveling anywhere on your own you plug straight in. Earphones in. Music playing. No one walks in silence anymore. And on the road up to the next town Simon definitely felt alone in that silence.

It was the afternoon. Aunt Bella had gone out. Uncle Aled was fishing.

Simon looked out over the sea and spotted half a dozen boats out there. He wondered if any of them could see him walking along up here. The good weather was continuing. The sun was hidden just behind the clouds. The wind had started to pick back up.

Simon was following the road. It snaked along the edge of the cliff following all of the bends and dips of the land. He found himself walking on the grass bank between the tarmac and the sheer drop down to the sea. Barely any cars drove past leaving Simon alone with the sounds of the water and wind. One sloshing, the other whistling quietly.

Now that he was up on top of the cliff he could see all of the coast as it meandered to the horizon. Ahead of him, three or four beaches away, Simon could make out the proverbial Next-Town-Along where hopefully a supermarket would make itself apparent. Beyond that a telephone mast stretched into the sky blinking a lazy red light at him, mocking the emptiness of his pocket.

Simon peered over his shoulder at the coast behind him. Past his tiny town, tucked in the valley, was nothing other than farmland. The white-walled graveyard just about poked into view over a hill. Further beyond that was a farm with an old yellowing caravan parked at under a tree in one of the fields. Simon could just about make out a figure stood outside, shirtless by the looks of it.

A car roared past, making Simon jump.

He was starting to regret not taking the bike.

***

As it turned out the supermarket couldn't have been easier to find. The main road cut straight through the middle of town. On either side of it was a school, a retirement home, an old bookshop and the supermarket. Every other building in the town was a house, each planted by small roads that stretched off the main one like a spider's web.

The automatic doors squeaked open. Directly inside stood a guy who could have been anywhere between twenty and thirty five. His hairline started at the very top of his head. What hair he had remaining was greasy. He was even skinnier than Simon and his uniform hung off him like snags of wool on a barbed wire fence. When he spoke the ratty mustache above his thin lips writhed up and down like a dying insect.

'Tourist?'

'I'm sorry?'

'You a tourist? Ain't seen you round before.'

'No, I um…'

Simon stopped himself. This man could be his employer. He plastered on a big smile and, against his better judgement, stretched out a hand in greeting.

'My name's Simon. I just moved in with my aunt and uncle near here. I was wondering if you have any job vacancies.'

The man stared at Simon's hand until he lowered it back to his side awkwardly. He then stretched out his own for Simon to shake. It was slightly damp.

'Aight, you'll wanna talk to Charlotte behind the till.'

'Brilliant, thank you.'

As Simon walked away it took all of his willpower not to wipe his hand on his jeans.

'Excuse me, are you Charlotte?'

The round woman behind the till looked up at him. Chewing gum and a magazine. She couldn't have been more stereotypical if she tried. When she spoke it was in a Welsh accent so heavy that Simon almost though she was speaking another language.

'Oo's askin? Cus if you wan a refund or sum-eh we don do none a them no more.'

'Hi, I'm Simon. I just moved to the area. I heard you might have a job vacancy for me?'

She sighed and rolled up her magazine. Glaring over Simon's shoulder at the weaselly man in the doorway it took Simon a second to realise she was still talking to him.

'You wan Phil. S'out back righ now I reckon.'

Simon smiled and nodded at her but he doubted she noticed. She was still too busy glaring at the man by the door.

There was an open door at the back of the supermarket which Simon took to be 'out back'. Outside was a man about as old and hard as the cliffs themselves. He was smoking as Simon approached him.

'Excuse me, I…'

'Break.'

'I'm sorry?'

'On break. Don't talk to me.'

'Oh, um. Right. It's just I was told-'

'Break.'

'Break. Right, sure.'

Simon sidled back inside. Charlotte didn't look up. The man from the door was gone. Simon was weighing his options whether to leave or not when a voice made him jump.

'So. About this job.'

It was the weaselly man from by the door. He had popped up from behind the freezer where he must have been crouched. He was now attempting to casually sit on it.

'I thought you said to talk to Charlotte?'

'And Charlotte sent you to Phil.'

'Yeah.'

'And just like that you've learned something key about business.'

'Um. Okay?'

'What did you learn?'

'Is this an interview?'

'What d'you learn, boy?'

'Um… that no one takes responsibility for things?'

'Exac- no! Seriously? Of course not. No. No, you learned the concept of hierarchy. Or rather, the lack thereof.'

'Okay?'

'See, I don't *believe* in traditional business structures. Not me, not at all. Because hierarchy means all of the responsibility falls on the people at the top. You know what I mean? You remember the financial crisis, boy?'

'Sure.'

'Well, who got in trouble for that?'

'Didn't they all get away with it?'

'No! The men at the top got in trouble. Sorry, the *people* at the top. And that's not fair is it? It wasn't their fault, was it?'

'I mean… no?'

'Exactly, see now you're getting it. Aren't you?'

'Sure.'

'Here, we don't believe in bosses. I mean, technically we do because I'm branch manager and get paid more than them. *But* they don't see me as a boss, they see me as a friend. Right Charlotte?'

Charlotte raised a fat thumbs up without lifting her eyes from the magazine.

'See?'

'I think so.'

'I'm *sharing* the responsibility. Everyone should be their own boss here.'

'If everyone's their own boss then surely that means you're not needed here though.'

The mustache scowled. There was a line of sweat along it.

'Do you want the job or not?'

'Um, yeah I guess I do.'

'Well, that ain't good enough, you hear? You've got to be begging for this job, you understand? I only take on employees who are 110% committed, you know.'

Simon glanced at Charlotte. He couldn't tell if she was still awake or not.

'I do want it... um, sir.'

'That's better. Still not good enough though. Here, take my number. Give me a ring when you feel like grovelling.'

He handed Simon a handwritten business card. Card was the wrong word, it felt more like printer paper.

Mr. Aaron Steel.

'Is that actually your name?'

The weasel looked flustered.

'Of course, it's my name!'

'Right.'

'It is.'

'Sure.'

Simon shoved the paper in his pocket and walked back out of the squeaky automatic doors.

***

'Like an actual caterpillar on his lip.'

'You're joking.'

'I swear on my life.'

Simon couldn't help but smile hearing his mum laughing out of the tinny receiver. The landline in the cottage looked like it had been purchased before he was born.

'So what's the plan? Are you going to take the job?'

'I don't know.'

'What other options have you got?'

'Literally nothing. Aunt Bella made it pretty clear she doesn't want me working in the pub.'

'Well, after everything with Huw…'

'I know.'

Neither of them said anything for a moment. The gravestone up on the cliff flashed through Simon's head. It was sat too close to the edge.

'Was it Bella who found you this job?'

'No, it wasn't actually.'

'Quelle surprise. How'd you hear about it then?'

'Oh it was just some girl.'

'Whoa, whoa, whoa. A *girl*?'

'Don't even start.'

'I said nothing. What's her name?'

'Mum.'

'How did you meet?'

'Mum, I will hang up the phone right now.'

'Okay, okay! No need to get so antsy, I just didn't expect to hear wedding bells so soon.'

'I'm hanging up.'

'I'll stop! I'm sorry.'

'If you must know, I really don't like her and I'm pretty sure she hates me.'

'She likes you enough to get you a job.'

'A job with five cons for every pro.'

'Everybody starts somewhere. When I was your age…'

'Here we go.'

'Fine, I'll spare you the lecture… How's the phone?'

'Broken. Like properly broken.'

'Hm… I tell you what, I'll let you come home when you can afford a new one. How does that sound?'

'Wait, really?'

'Yeah sure. I think that sounds fair.'

'What's to stop me getting a ten pound brick?'

'Would you get a ten pound brick?'

'Good point.'

'Buy a phone. Then you can get on the first train out of Cardiff.'

'You sure you don't want to give me a bigger challenge here?'

'Well, of course I expect you to be a gentleman and pay rent to your aunt and uncle.'

'Okay.'

'And cover food.'

'Sure.'

'And petrol.'

'But after all that, once I get a new phone I can come home?'

'I don't see why not.'

'Well in that case, I guess this supermarket job is my best bet.'

'You better get grovelling, boy.'

'I'll try my best. Love you mum.'

'I love you too. Send my love to Bella and Aled.'

Simon hung up the phone and picked it back up, pausing with his fingers over the buttons. The business card was sat on the table next to him. It was hard to read the numbers in that awful font. Aaron Steel picked up on the second ring.

'Aight?'

'Hello, it's Simon. From earlier.'

'Oh right, yeah. You.'

'Yeah, me. Um, about that job.'

''Ere it comes.'

'I was just wondering if the vacancy was still open.'

He could hear Aaron sucking in air between his teeth on the other end.

'''At depends.'

'On what?'

'On what you learned.'

Simon bit his lip to stop himself saying the first thing that came to mind. He'd practiced this. He tried to fill his voice with as much contempt as he could.

'I've learned that there is something more important in business than numbers, products, and profits.'

'Oh yeah?'

'Something that makes more than just a good businessman. Something that makes a good man.'

'And what's that?'

Simon held the receiver away from his face for a moment with his eyes closed. In a voice that he hoped had as much sarcasm in it as humanly possible he continued.

'Soul. A heart for those around him. To respect them, the love them and… to forgive them.'

'8am tomorrow.'

'Yeah?'

'Welcome to the family, Simpson.'

'It's Simon.'

'I know.'

The line went dead. Simon had never imagined a smug mustache before but he was pretty certain there was one somewhere on the Welsh coast tonight.

***

'Are you sure you don't want to take my bike?'

'Really, it's fine. I'm happy walking.'

'It's quite a long way, sweetie.'

'I walked there and back yesterday just fine.'

'Okay, well if you change your mind you can always take it tomorrow.'

'Thank you.'

Aunt Bella smiled and took hold of Simon's oversized sleeves. He couldn't help but smile back even if he was still half asleep.

'I um, I really appreciate everything.'

'We're happy to have you.'

'As soon as I get paid I'll give you some rent money and start covering my costs.'

He paused, waiting for her to argue and tell him that he was family and didn't have to pay anything. She just smiled again and tugged his sleeves down before sending him out into the wind.

***

The walk seemed even longer the second time around, the way all long journeys do. Something about the human memory makes it really difficult to actually imagine durations properly. You feel like you must be halfway there, look at your watch and realise you've only been going for ten minutes.

Simon sighed and shrugged against the weather. Aunt Bella was still dressing him in those awful jumpers but this morning, when no one could see him, he was quietly glad to have it. He couldn't tell whether it was sea mist in the air of really fine rain. He supposed there wasn't that much of a difference when the wind's this strong. It was just cold and wet. He couldn't see it, but boy could he feel it.

His cheeks felt raw. He reckoned he must have been glowing like a toddler who's spent too much time at the park in winter. He tried to do the maths as he walked, to figure out how many times he'd have to make this journey to and from work before he could escape back to London.

He reckoned he'd be on minimum wage here so about £5.90. If he did nine hour days that would be around £53 a day, fingers crossed they'd pay his lunch break. He had no clue what the rent prices in the area would be but he reckoned £90 a week would cover that. So he was already £90 in debt. Then on top of that he'd have to figure out fuel prices from Cardiff where Uncle Aled and Aunt Bella had picked him up from. Oh and then fuel prices for the smaller journeys. Then food costs, those hopefully wouldn't be too bad.

A car roared past and splashed him sending cold water all the way up the right side of his body. For a moment the cold knocked all of the air out of his lungs. His clothes felt heavy when he started walking again.

He had to start the maths all over again but it didn't take long to catch back up. He didn't reckon he'd actually have to stay here too long. £500 for a phone was a decent bar to aim for. Plus he'd probably have to get his train ticket back home as well. He'd be making around £265 a week minus maybe £120 or so in expenses. So that would be…

A month? Something like that.

Okay. He could probably deal with that. Right? A month isn't so long. If he factored in the time he had already done that put him 20% of the way through his time in Wales already.

The thought almost made Simon smile into the rain. His pace picked up as the town came into view.

***

'You're late.'

'I'm sorry?'

'You're late. See that clock on the wall?'

7:56

'You said to be here at 8.'

'First rule of business, always be early.'

'I am early.'

'At least five minutes early.'

Simon closed his mouth. Just one month.

'Okay, I'm sorry. I'll be on time tomorrow. I mean early, I'll be early tomorrow.'

'Good. You've learned the second rule of business: always learn. It's something I still practice everyday, believe it or not.'

Aaron's mustache curled upwards as the corners. It was slick with rainwater.

'So, um. What's my first task?'

'Tasks? No, no, no, we don't have tasks here.'

'We don't?'

'No, no. Missions, boy. What's your first mission?'

'Okay then, what's my first mission?'

'Bins. Take 'em out.'

'Brilliant.'

Just one month.

***

The bag split open when Simon was halfway to the bin. The rain that had been like a fine mist earlier was now fat and heavy. Each drop slapped his head as he knelt on the tarmac gingerly picking up unrecognisable food remnants. A small part of him was praying they'd give him a dry uniform when he got back inside. Somehow he reckoned there'd be a few hoops to jump through before Aaron gave him the holiest of holy robes though.

Simon tossed the last of the rotting fruit into the bin and turned to head back in. Leaning next to the door, under the only square foot of rain cover, was the guy from before who'd been smoking. He was smoking again. It wouldn't have surprised Simon if the man hadn't left this spot since the two had last met. What was his name again? Phil, right?

'Thanks for the help.'

'On break.'

'Of course you are.'

Back inside Aaron was waiting for Simon by the till. A sneer on his face. Or that might have just been his normal face.

'Simpson, over here. You know how to work one of these things?'

Simon sidled round behind the counter and looked at the till. In about 3 seconds flat he reckoned he knew how it worked.

'Sure. Doesn't look too complicated.'

'Ever used one before?'

'No, I can't say I have.'

Aaron sighed.

'Looks like I'll have to give you a run through.'

'I mean, it looks easy enough.'

'Pen.'

'Sorry?'

'Pen! Where's your pen and your notepad?'

'I, I didn't bring any.'

'Are you shittin' me, boy?'

'I didn't think I'd need them.'

'Rule 3 of business.'

'Always have a notepad and pen?'

'Always have a notepad and goddamn pen. Go to aisle three. Now.'

Simon quickly found a rack of stationary and grabbed what he needed. He paused, trying to level his head.

'Boy?'

'Coming.'

'Those are straight out of your first paycheck, you got it?'

'Yes, sir.'

Just one month.

Aaron looked like he didn't know whether to be furious or gleeful. He was the sheriff in these parts and he was getting to chink around in his spurs for the first time in a long time. Simon knew he was making it too easy for the man.

They spent twenty minutes at the till. Simon would roleplay as a customer, Aaron would operate the till. Then Aaron would roleplay as the customer and Simon would operate the till, all while taking notes, learning the fourth, fifth, sixth, and seventh rules of business, and doing his best not to see the pen in his hand as a potential murder weapon.

'Now boy, you see all the money in this till?'

'Yeah?'

'It ain't yours. I count every penny of it myself. You good at maths Simpson?'

'I'm alright, I guess.'

'I'm better, okay? Don't try to outsmart me here. Understand?'

'I won't steal anything, don't worry.'

'Good. Any given day we could have over £10,000 in here.'

'That doesn't seem very clever.'

'What did you say, boy?'

'I'm just saying, that's a lot of money to be stolen. Shouldn't you have a safe or something?'

'Who'd steal anything round here? The old folks across the road? Besides I *have* got a safe. It's in the back office under my desk. And nobody - *nobody* - is getting in that bad boy.'

'What do you mean *you've* got a safe?'

'It's my safe.'

'So it's your money in there? Then why's it here?'

'Because... well, because I need it okay? F-for tax reasons.'

Simon raised his eyebrows. Aaron had gone bright red. Sweat slicked his moustache.

'Look, if you must know, sometimes, as a business owner, I need to invest the uh, the revenues of the business into external sources.'

'Are these revenues being picked out of the tills?'

'Sometimes yes.'

'And these external sources are what?'

'They're none of your goddamn business, that's what. Now open the till again. We're doing this until you can do it blindfolded.'

Aaron wasn't joking about the blindfold.

'You ever seen Star Wars boy?'

'Yup.'

'You know who Master Yoda is?'

'Uh-huh.'

'And Luke Skywalker.'

'Yeah.'

'Good.'

Aaron left such a long pause that Simon thought that was the end of that conversation.

'Think of us like them. You're running round in training, learning to lift X-Wings with the force.'

'And you're always on my back.'

'And I've always got your back, exactly. See? You're learning. Just like rule 3 says.'

'Rule 2.'

'You wanna know rule 8, boy? Don't be smart-arse.'

Simon took extra care writing that one down in his notepad.

***

Mercifully, Aaron disappeared at around lunchtime leaving Simon alone behind the till. Over the course of the entire working day he saw maybe five customers. Given this was the only supermarket in the area he imagined this place must be teeming on weekends, but on a Tuesday afternoon it was practically deserted. One lady who'd come in spoke to him for a bit. She was a teacher at the school across the road. She'd given Simon a flier for the upcoming village fete that was being held over in the school. The words *Fancy Dress* and *Egg Hunt* immediately put him off but he'd carefully tucked the flier into his notepad anyway just to be polite.

Charlotte sat reading magazines. Every time she finished one she would walk over to the shelf and pick out the next one. Phil would either sit on a stool by the back door or stand two feet outside of it smoking. No one spoke. No one did anything. Simon just sat behind the till flicking tiny balls of paper into the bin. No one had told him that a clock could move this slow. Every time he looked up at it, the minute hand would have only moved along a couple of notches, no matter how long Simon felt he had waited.

4:58

So close. Simon flicked his last piece of paper into the bin and sat watching the clock. He'd forgotten how long two minutes felt when you had no headphones in, no videos to watch, no screen to stare at.

4:59

Close enough. Simon stood up, cracked his spine, stretched his arms above his head and made for the door.

'Bye, guys. I'll see you tomorrow.'

Neither Charlotte or Phil acknowledged him as the automatic doors squeaked open and the wind sprayed him down with icy cold rainwater.

***

'I told you to take a coat.'

Simon was fairly certain Aunt Bella hadn't told him that. There was an air of smugness about her when he walked into the porch, dripping water all over the welcome mat. She'd proven a point to him somehow. But what was it? To always bring a raincoat? That Welsh boys needed to be tougher? Simon was too wet and tired to figure it out. He tried to step forward but Aunt Bella blocked his path.

'Oh no you don't, sweetie. I just cleaned the house today.'

'Okay. What should I do then?'

'Here.'

She handed him a towel and Simon smiled genuinely for the first time in what felt like an age.

'Good day?'

Simon toweled off his hair before replying.

'Um, not exactly.'

'Oh?'

'Do you know the manager at the supermarket? A guy named Aaron?'

'I know *of* him.'

'Yeah, well we don't really see eye to eye.'

'On some things?'

'On anything.'

'Ah.'

'Yeah, I think it'll be alright though. I'll just try to be patient.'

'That's a very mature thing to say.'

He knew she meant it well but it just came across as patronising.

'I'm gonna go change. I've been in these wet clothes all day.'

'Dinner's in twenty.'

***

The evening went by way too quickly. Before Simon knew it he was in bed staring at the ceiling. He reached out to check the time on his phone but it wasn't there. Of course it wasn't. All that was on his bedside table was that pair of damn walkie-talkies. They were a sweet present, they really were, but right now they only made him feel worse. He felt like a kid with a tin can telephone but no sibling to share it with.

Who did he actually know in this town?

His aunt and uncle. The vicar. Aaron.

Maisie.

Simon rolled over. It made sense why she told him about the job now. She must've known how miserable it would be. She'd probably be in there in a couple of days time to gloat.

The door to the pub crashed open again. Simon checked the time. It was already 1am. Only five hours until he'd have to get up for work. The urge to smother himself in his pillow was a strong one. Having been tired all evening he was wide awake now. He couldn't sleep and that'd frustrated him. The frustration had got his blood pumping and properly woken him up.

He kicked off the duvet and walked over to the window. There was none of the warm orange glow of streetlights you'd get back home. Just darkness. Only one chink of yellow light broke up the black streets. It was falling out of the open pub door and stretching out on the pavement like a Hopper painting.

Simon watched as a man with a mess of short curly hair, tied up out of his eyes, paced back and forth cutting across it, taking furious drags from his cigarette. He was clenching and unclenching his fists in time with his steps. He looked like a bull in its cage before it was sent out into the ring. He only wearing a vest despite the sky drizzling rain onto his shoulders.

As if on queue a figure appeared in the illuminated door and threw a jacket out on the floor. The two shouted indistinctly as one another for a moment before the man staggered over to the jacket, threw it over his wet shoulders and spat on the pub's doormat. Seemingly proud of himself he strode off into the night. Argument already forgotten he was now a carefree drunk, staggering towards the coastal path, singing 'Baa Baa Black Sheep' at the top of his lungs.

And with that the man disappeared from view, the pub door swung shut and Simon returned to bed where he lay awake for another hour before sleep finally took him.

Chapter 5

Simon only really came to his senses halfway through stacking a shelf the next day. For the first time since the previous night he felt fully conscious. Running on that weird autopilot that only comes with sleep deprivation, he had somehow got up, showered, dressed, borrowed Aunt Bella's bike, cycled all the way to work, held a conversation with Aaron, and sat at the till for an hour. It was only now, as he stared at the barcode on a pot of yoghurt that he felt himself taking over his brain again.

He rubbed his eyes and let out a long yawn. Glancing up at the clock on the wall he saw it was only 8:45. Aaron was whistling a tune that seemed to consist of only one note repeated over and over again. He'd already done a day. Just a few more of them left.

'Simpson?'

'Yeah?'

There was no point arguing about his name. The more he did it, the more he played into Aaron's greasy little hands.

'You know what day it is?'

'Wednesday.'

'Delivery day, boy. Better start limbering up.'

'What delivery?'

'New fridge. Gonna go right over there.'

He pointed at the shelf Simon had just finished filling.

'But there's already a shelf there.'

'Well well, it looks like you might be right about that boy. Since you're such a clever lad, how's about you deal with that little problem for me?'

Simon bit his lip.

'Oh and uh, I'll be going out when the fridge arrives and Phil ain't in today so...'

'So the delivery guy will have to move it in?'

Aaron just laughed and bit down on a fresh stick of gum.

***

As it turned out, there was no delivery man. It was a woman about three inches shorter than Simon who pulled up in the van and made him sign for the fridge. Between the two of them they managed to shift the monstrosity onto a trolley that was missing a wheel. It kept tipping onto its side and threatened to throw the fridge on the floor in protest any second.

By the time the fridge was in place it was already half an hour later than Simon was supposed to be working. He was still yet to plug it in and get the thing working. Charlotte half watched the fiasco but soon returned her gaze back to the much more intriguing depths of her magazine.

All told, by the time Simon was ready to head home it was fully dark outside and raining again. He could barely see across the street as he unlocked his bike from a lamppost. The old bookshop was the only other place still open. Simon thought he saw a someone moving around inside but that was probably his imagination. No one ever really went in there as far as he could tell.

Aunt Bella's bike was... well, it was Aunt Bella in bike form. It was about as traditional of a ladies bike as they come. There was even a basket. Simon swung it around and faced it back down the road heading out of town. It was only about a twenty minute ride but there was a hell of an incline to start off with.

Simon had decided very quickly that he hated this bike. He'd never been the most confident cyclist but on this thing he struggled not to tumble off at every opportunity. There were no gears to change. You got your one Welsh gear and you stuck with it whether you were crawling uphill or shooting down. And the best part? No brakes. You had to pedal backwards to slow it down.

The bike rattled as Simon pushed off. There was a squeak of protest from the wet chain. When he glanced down to look at it his foot slipped off the pedal and sharp metal cut into his calf. The bike wobbled and he pulled over at the side of the road and stuck his foot directly in a puddle.

Simon swore. Loudly.

By the time he'd got going properly he realised that there were no street lights lining the road as it wound between towns. All of his route up onto and along the cliffs would be in total darkness. In the rain. On Aunt Bella's bike.

The road started to curve upwards. The fire started to burn through Simon's legs, clashing horribly with the freezing rainwater soaking his trousers. Neither sensation balanced the other out. He was already exhausted from having to lug the fridge around for the last hour and so he'd barely made it onto the hill when his legs started to feel like spaghetti.

Just one month, right? He only had to make this journey for once month. Well, he'd have to make it twice a day so that was kind of like doing two months.

Mercifully there was a little dip before the actual hill. The road was now completely black. There was a turn coming up but he couldn't quite make out where. Simon stood up on the pedals, letting the bike free wheel and pick up some speed before reaching the next hill. If he could just-

Tarmac smacked him in the face. His back arched over his head. The road clawed at his face. Then grass. Then he was tumbling. Over once. Over twice. Then the ditch caught him and held him down in a wet muddy hug.

For a long time Simon didn't move. The water was icy cold and he could feel himself slowly sinking into the mud. Rain pattered against his back. He was definitely bleeding from his face, maybe other places too. He'd never broken a bone before and so he didn't want to move any limbs in case he'd just changed that.

The grass bank in front of him lit up. A set of tires were roaring up the road behind him. Just as the lights were about to shine onto his face there was a screeching sound and the unmistakable sound of metals grinding against tarmac. The lights danced up and then back down as the same noise came again in quick succession. Then the car rounded the corner and continued up the hill as if nothing had happened.

After a few more seconds, when Simon finally came to terms with the fact that no one was coming to help him up, he planted a hand in the mud and pushed himself up. There was an audible squelch as his aching body rose out of the water and stumbled up the bank. He was moving at least. If something was broken, he'd know by now.

Both knees and elbows were throbbing dully. He wiped what he hoped was muddy water out of his eyes and looked down at the bike. The car had bent it completely out of shape. The frame had a crack running along it, both wheels were folded almost in half and the handlebars were twisted into a cruel S shape.

Simon could just about make out a pair of tail lights as they crested the hill and disappeared into the night. The supermarket was still right there. He'd made it maybe 200 meters before hitting the pothole and ruining the bike. Thunder rumbled somewhere overhead.

A wave hit the rocks so hard that it managed to peek over the edge of the cliff at Simon as he stood next to the ruined bike.

***

Aunt Bella screamed when Simon walked through the door. The noise cut right through his pounding head. It sounded like something out of a horror film. She rushed over to him and started babbling.

'My goodness! What happened? Simon, sweetie. You're covered in blood. Did you get hit by a car? Where's the bike? Forget the bike. Are you okay? Where does it hurt? Did anyone stop to help you? Should I call an ambulance?'

'Aunt B-'

'Sh! Don't speak, you might be concussed. I'll run and get the bandages and we'll take you to hospital right away. No, we'll call an ambulance. Which is quicker? No don't answer that. How would you know?'

'Aunt Bella.'

'Come and sit down. Unless it's your spine. Is it your spine? Can you walk? I mean you can stand, right? Of course you can. You already are. Okay. You just stand there then and I'll...'

'Aunt Bella, I-'

'Oh, Simon. What am I going to tell your mother? Should I call her now? She's probably worrying already. Mothers know, they always...'

She stopped suddenly. Uncle Aled's hand had appeared on her shoulder. It seemed to suck all of the panic out of her and for a moment no one said a word. When Uncle Aled spoke his voice was as placid as ever.

'Bella. Go run a bath.'

She was panting, looking at him. Her shoulders dropped.

'A bath, yes. A bath. I'll go and run a bath. Okay.'

She pottered away leaving Simon and his uncle alone by the front door. Uncle Aled turned and walked into the kitchen. Simon followed.

There was a first aid kit in one of the cupboards that Uncle Aled got down and placed on the kitchen table. Simon sat in an empty chair and Uncle Aled pulled another one over to face him. There was a sound of running water somewhere in the house.

'What hurts?'

'My head, mostly. I mean everywhere kind of hurts but I think it's mostly bruises.'

Uncle Aled got to work cleaning Simon's face and dabbing at the cuts with a small bit of cotton wool. The house was mostly dark except for the light hanging over the kitchen table. The cuts on his face stung but Simon tried not to show it. Uncle Aled pulled out a little torch and shone it in each of Simon's eyes, nodding slightly as he did.

'Have a bath.'

'Okay.'

'Simon.'

Uncle Aled paused for a long time. Simon watched as he tried to find the right words.

'It's good… that you are okay.'

Simon nodded. The two of them looked at each other. Uncle Aled's mouth scrunched up. He was smiling. In his own quiet little way.

***

Simon couldn't sleep again.

The cuts on his face had reopened as soon as he lay down and so he'd spent a while dabbing them with a wet cloth to not get any blood on the pillow case. He couldn't find a comfortable position. His back ached, his ankle was swollen and both of his arms were stiff from the shoulder blade all the way down to his finger tips.

The bath had helped. The warm water was a welcome relief from the wet clothes that he'd been wearing all day. His wounds stung as he lowered himself into the tub It was a good pain. By the time he'd assessed his injuries, washed all of the mud off and climbed out of the bath, the water was a reddish brown with flecks of blood clots and dirt floating on the surface.

But now that he was in bed all of his muscles had seized up. Any which way he rested at least one of his limbs started hurting. There was no use trying to sleep through it.

He would have gone on his phone. Instead he just lay there in the darkness staring up at the yellow ceiling. Even the pub was quiet tonight.

Seconds ticked into minutes.

Minutes ticked into hours.

The black sky outside faded into a cool blue.

A soft knock came from the door.

'Sweetie?'

Simon swung his legs around and climbed to his feet. His bare feet made a small padding noise as he walked over to the door. Aunt Bella's concerned expression met him when it swung open.

'I'm okay. It's not as bad as it looks.'

'Did you sleep well?'

'Pretty well, yeah.'

The concern on her face softened slightly.

'Well you just stay in bed today, okay? I can call in sick for you.'

'I'm going to work.'

'Sweetie…'

'I'm fine, trust me. If Uncle Aled gives me a lift we can stop off and get the bike from where I left it.'

'Are you sure?'

Simon put his hands lightly on her shoulders and met her gaze head-on.

'I'm fine.'

'Okay. I'll go and wake Aled.'

He was going to work and that was that.

Just one month.

'Oh and Simon, sweetie?'

'Yeah?'

'Take a walkie-talkie with you. Aled and I will keep the other one.'

Simon nodded. He reckoned he didn't have much choice.

***

'Jesus Christ, Simpson. What happened?'

'Simon.'

'You what?'

'My *name* is Simon.'

They glared at one another over the counter. Simon watched the ratty little mustache twitch.

'You good to work?'

'Of course I am.'

'You ain't got a concussion?'

'Would you care if I did?'

'Of course. Legally speaking.'

'Well?'

'Well what?'

'Well what am I doing today? Working the till?'

'We got shelves what need stacking. You can do that, Mr Schwarzenegger.'

Aaron's mouth curled. He was clearly very proud of himself for that joke.

And so Simon spent the morning stacking shelves. Normally it would have been done in maybe an hour but Simon was working at half speed on account of all the bruises slowly painting him purple beneath the uniform. Charlotte peered over at him for a whole two seconds before going back to her magazine. Phil gave him an approving smile.

Simon was just placing the last multipack of Walker's on the shelf when he heard the automatic doors squeak open. He turned back to the trolley to start unloading the rice cakes. He didn't want any conversations with the local biddies about his face. He'd had enough sympathetic looks from Aunt Bella already. There was a small gasp, quickly stifled. Whoever it was must have just seen the scratches. Simon couldn't help but feel tough.

Simon cast a nonchalant glance over in the direction of the sound and froze. Dressed in an ugly oversized jumper with her long tangly hair stood Maisie, holding a bag of brioche and some raisins. Simon looked back at the trolley quickly. He could pretend he hadn't seen her right? Except he'd been stood stock still for a couple of seconds now.

Damn it.

'What's the other guy look like?'

He'd forgotten how annoying her accent was.

Simon shrugged and started stacking the shelf again. He wasn't paying attention to what items he was putting where. She didn't leave. Simon noticed that the black eye she'd been sporting on Sunday had gone down a bit.

'I could ask you the same thing.'

Maisie played with her sleeve.

'You got the job then?'

'Yup.'

She sidled over to him. Leaning against the shelf, hands behind her back, she tried to catch Simon's eye but he pretended to be reading one of the item descriptions.

'You gonna say thanks?'

'For what?'

'I don't know, your employment?'

'Well, I hate working here so I guess you got what you wanted.'

Maisie let out a dramatic sigh and started walking away.

'You know, I'm not a bad person.'

Just as she said that a bag of rice cakes fell out of the back of her jumper. Then two snickers and a chicken wrap.

'It's not what it looks like.'

Simon didn't say anything. Oh this was good. This was really good. She couldn't have been any redder handed. Finally he had something to gloat about. He raised an eyebrow and closed the gap between them. Maisie started whispering frantically.

'Look, I was gonna get a basket but I forgot so I thought I could just carry them in my jumper. I woulda got them out again at the till. I was gonna pay for it. Look, I've got the money, see? I was just picking up some groceries. Besides, who'd want to steal from here?'

'Maisie.'

'I'm not a thief. I *swear* I ain't no thief.'

'Oh sure. I believe you.'

'See? We're all good then.'

'The question is whether Phil believes you.'

Simon nodded his head towards the back door where Phil had just walked in. Maisie's face dropped.

'Alright, fine. I was nicking a few things. But what are you gonna do about it? Like really, what will *you* do? I've seen you with your aunt, you just do everything she tells you to. You're a pushover and you know it. I'm gonna walk out of this shop right now with this food up my jumper and you're just gonna keep stacking that shelf.'

There was a glint in Maisie's eye though. She didn't look entirely sure of herself. Maybe she was right. Maybe most days Simon would have stood back and let her leave. What did he care? He didn't have any loyalties to this place. If anything he disliked it here. But today Simon's face was too scratched up to relax. And you know what? He was done. He was done with all of it.

'You have ten seconds to pay me or I call Phil.'

'No.'

'Nine.'

'You really think that'll work on me?'

'Eight.'

'Mate, I'm not a five year old. There's no naughty step to…'

'Seven.'

'Alright, fine. How much?'

'£30.'

'Piss off.'

'Six.'

'Not happening.

'Five.'

'Not happening.'

'Four.'

'£20.'

'Three.'

'£25.'

'Two.'

'Alright fine. You dickhead. I'll give you the damn money.'

Maisie reached into the pocket of her jeans and pulled a fat wallet. It was stuffed so full Simon was surprised it wasn't spilling money onto the floor. She pulled out three scrunched tens and shoved them against Simon's chest right on a bruise. He winced.

'How much money is that?'

'£30 like you asked.'

'No, in your wallet.'

'I ain't telling you! Just take yours and be happy. Don't spend it all at once or whatever.'

'Where did you get all that?'

'We're done here.'

'Maisie, that's like a thousand pounds.'

'Alright, we are not on first name terms.'

The wallet was back in her pocket. She made it to the automatic doors before Simon caught up. Something had sparked in his mind.

'Where do you work?'

'I don't. I do a few favours for a few people.'

'You sell drugs?'

'What? No. Of course I don't.'

Simon raised his eyebrows.

'You seriously think I sell drugs? Round here? You reckon they're blowing trees through between games of bingo? Oh, I've really got the munchies. Here I'll pop a couple Werther's. Let me get the false teeth out and rub crack on my gums.'

'Alright, then what is it? How do you make money?'

'I'm not saying.'

'Because it's illegal?'

'Because I'm not saying.'

'I won't snitch on you.'

'Yeah, sure you won't.'

Simon grabbed her arm. It was smaller than he expected.

'I won't tell. Okay?'

The two met eyes for a moment. The sting went out of both of them.

'Why do you care so much?'

'Because I hate working here. I hate stacking shelves, I hate my boss, I hate being bored, I hate this town, I hate almost everyone in it. I just want to make some money and go home.'

'Huh.'

'I want to be back in London where I have friends and I have a life and no one's treating me like a baby. I… I just want to go home.'

'And you need money to do that.'

'Exactly. Look, I don't know what you do. I don't really care. But I can help you. No, no, don't give me that face. Hear me out okay? I'll help you with it. Just split the money fairly with me and I'll do my absolute best.'

'And how exactly d'you reckon you can help me?'

Simon paused for a moment, choosing his words carefully.

'I'm good with numbers.'

'I'm leaving.'

'Maisie, wait. You want a proper answer? Look, everyone here trusts me but I don't think any of them trust you.'

Maisie didn't say anything for a long time. She was a couple of inches shorter than Simon. For the first time, standing in close proximity to her, Simon properly realised that she was a girl, a real girl, who was his age. He felt stupid.

'Fine. Meet me tomorrow at the beach. 7am.'

'What really? Just like that?'

'D'you want me to change my mind?'

'I'll be there. 7am. Got it. God, does anyone in this town ever have a lie in?'

Maisie almost smiled at him.

'The early bird and all that. You don't have a phone anymore, do you?'

Simon shook his head. His hand reached instinctively for his right pocket. There was something in it.

'I've uh, I've got walkie-talkies.'

Maisie did smile now. It was the kind of smile you make when someone wants to watch a Disney movie and you have to pretend for a moment that you're too old for that before saying yes.

'Here, take this one. The other one's back home. Don't use it until I call you first, okay?'

Maisie nodded and put the walkie-talkie in her back pocket.

'So this is happening then?'

'I guess it is.'

Just like that, things were suddenly just as awkward as when she'd first arrived. Friends would have probably hugged here and said goodbye but Simon didn't dare try that. He want to hug her anyway. So what were they? Business partners. What do business partners do? Shake hands?

'Alright, bye.'

Maisie turned and walked out of the automatic doors before Simon settled on anything. He walked back inside and grabbed a sandwich off the shelf.

For a while he stood by the automatic doors eating. They slid open for him giving him a view of the world outside whenever he moved. The sky was clear and the sunlight was dancing off the wet road. A cloud roll overhead. Simon tilted his head round and called back inside.

'Hey Aaron.'

'Yeah, what? Make it quick I'm busy.'

'Alright. I quit.'

And with that Simon strode out through the doors, eating a sandwich.

***

He couldn't tell Aunt Bella. He definitely couldn't tell his mum. For all intents and purposes he'd have to act as if he was still working at the supermarket and just hope that whatever Maisie had him doing didn't arouse too much attention. That meant that he had about four hours to kill until he could head home.

For a while Simon just walked up the coastal path. The ground under his feet shone from the previous night's rain. The sea was gentle enough today. From up at the top of the cliffs it just sounded like one long hushing sound. An elderly couple walked past Simon and smiled at him. He still couldn't get used to that. Back home you didn't look at anyone, let alone smile at a complete stranger.

He didn't care too much about getting mud on his uniform. He didn't reckon he'd ever be wearing it again and he had half a mind to get it as muddy as possible before handing it back to Aaron. He stopped on a little grass bank that sloped off towards the cliff edge. Huw's knitted jumper was tied around his waist. As ugly as it was, Simon couldn't bring himself to sit on it. Instead he tied the sleeves around a fencepost and watched it flap in the wind.

If only he could just live like this. Just existing out by the sea. Then he reckoned he'd enjoy life here a lot more. If he could just get up everyday when he wanted, come out onto the cliffside and just *be*. That'd be the life. Now that he thought about it, that's probably why everyone retired out here. He sat himself down on a rock.

He tried to close his eyes and relax but there was something small, like a knot drawn tight as possible, somewhere inside him. He'd just made a big mistake. He knew it. If Aaron had been hesitant to hire Simon before there was no way in hell he'd rehire him now. What's more he didn't even know Maisie at all. He'd had maybe two conversations with her and now he was trusting her enough to quit his job. He had no clue what they'd be doing the following morning, how much he'd get paid, whether he'd get in trouble, whether Aunt Bella or Uncle Aled would catch him, what his mum would say if she found out…

Maybe he should have just stuck it out at the supermarket. It was only a month after all. All of the maths he'd done to work out his time here had gone out of the window. He was now just as unemployed and just as uncertain of the future as when he'd first arrived.

Something warm and wet found his cheek. Hot dog breath filled Simon's nose. It was a golden retriever, one he'd seen a couple of times around town. Simon laughed and fell back into the grass playing with the dog until its owner called it away.

***

'Come on, Simon. Eat up.'

'It's delicious, thanks. I'm just not really that hungry.'

Aunt Bella was about to say more when Uncle Aled gave her a look. Simon pretended he didn't notice.

They'd gone out to look at the bike when Simon had got home, the three of them. The same thing had happened then too, Aunt Bella had been about to say something before Uncle Aled stepped in. Crashing the bike had somehow brought Simon's uncle over to his side. Maybe he felt sorry for Simon. Whatever it was, Simon preferred his uncle's pity to his aunt's. It was less condescending for sure.

It was pretty clear that the bike was beyond repair. Every part of it needed replacing. Simon offered to pay for a new one hoping that Aunt Bella would decline but she remained silent. After a moment Uncle Aled spoke up.

'No.'

And that settled that.

Gathered around the dinner table Simon danced around the questions about work until Aunt Bella gave up.

'How's your face, sweetie?'

'It's not too bad actually. It still stings if I move anything too much.'

'Are you sure you don't need to go to the hospital just in case?'

'No, I'm fine. I think I'll just get an early night tonight.'

'Okay but you promise to tell us if anything happens to you.'

Simon hesitated. *Well now that you mention it, I quit my job today to pursue a career in petty crime with a girl I can't stand.*

'Yeah. Of course I will.'

'Aled can give you a lift tomorrow again.'

'No. I'll go myself. You guys lie in.'

'It's a long walk.'

'I like the fresh air. It's good for the cuts too.'

'Hmm.'

'I'll be fine, honestly. And thanks for dinner, it really was delicious.'

The knot was still in Simon's stomach when he went to bed.

***

Once every eye in the town was closed and every head was sunken into a pillow, the world came to life. The trees pulled their spindly legs out of the ground and stretched with a yawn. Between their feet dashed the fallen leaves from all of the front gardens, running down to have a dip in the sea before anyone else got there.

Somewhere in the darkness a cat slid out of a flap, yowled, and shot back inside. The leaves froze, waiting to see if any lights came on, but none of the people stirred. After a minute or so of stillness they resumed their night out at the beach, keen to enjoy their break as much as they could before the sun came up and chased them back into position.

Somewhere out on the cliffs, a knitted jumper flapped against a fencepost.

Chapter 6

There was already a figure perched on a rock when Simon arrived on the beach. She was sitting with her feet folded up under her. She would have looked like a monk if it wasn't for the curly hair whipping this way and that in the wind. As he approached her she skimmed her last stone out across the water and watched it disappear into the grey. She jumped slightly when Simon called out to her.

'Morning.'

'Aight?'

'Yeah, not bad. You?'

Maisie sighed in answer and hopped down off her rock.

'You ready?'

'I still don't actually know what I'm supposed to be ready for?'

'You ever gone crabbing before?'

'When I was a kid, sure. Why?'

'Why d'you reckon?'

'What, seriously? That's how you make money?'

Maisie gave another more emphatic sigh and started walking. Despite being taller than her, Simon struggled to keep up. Her feet danced across the surface of the sand like it was nothing while his sank with every step.

'So, what do you do? Sell the crabs?'

'A'ight, first things first, shut up.'

'How can I help you if I don't know what we're doing?'

Maisie stopped so suddenly that Simon nearly walked right through her.

'Alright, right now you're being loud. Someone up them cliffs could hear every word you're saying right now. Keep your voice down and you'll figure it.'

Simon didn't reply. They kept walking, this time in silence.

They followed the water along. The tide was on its way out, slowly retreating further and further away from them with each wave. Simon veered off the sand to follow the path as it wound up the cliff but Maisie stayed by the water's edge, waiting.

'Aren't we going this way?'

'How many crabs do you reckon are up there?'

Simon face grew hot in the morning chill. He itched his nose, hoping to come off nonchalant. For some reason he always felt like Maisie could see right through him. He looked away from her and retraced his steps. A wave came up just far enough to brush the soles of her battered shoes as he joined her.

Maisie was watching something. She was staring at the rocks by the edge of the cliff. Simon tried to follow her line of sight but couldn't see anything. Dark seaweed coated the rocks and glistened in the cold glow of the early morning sun. For a while they just stood there, Maisie watching the rocks, Simon the sea. The clouds were hanging low over the water today, painting the whole world a tired grey. There were no boats to be seen.

All of a sudden, Maisie was no longer by his side. Her long hair was dancing up and down as she hopped from rock to rock, the water jumping up and swirling inches from her feet.

'Careful! They look slippery.'

Maisie halted, balancing expertly on one foot with the other leg extended behind her like a ballerina. Her head turned slowly towards him, a sour look on her face. Simon decided it was probably for the best not to warn her twice.

As if to prove her point, Maisie pivoted on the one foot and continued leaping from rock to rock even faster and even more accurately. Somehow she was managing to plant the toes of her Converses in the exact spot on each rock that would give her grip. Simon stood mesmerised. Waves would hit the rocks, leap up and Maisie would dance perfectly around them so that not a drop ever touched her clothes.

All of that elegance was contrasted by the look she threw back in Simon's direction as she landed on the furthest rock out. The rock was only a centimeter or so above the water, she must have been waiting for the tide to go out just far enough to leave that one exposed.

Maisie squatted down and dipped her hands into the sea. To Simon it looked like she was literally perched on the surface of the water. The waves lapped against her forearms as she felt around for something Simon couldn't see. She steadied herself and with a small amount of effort hauled a seaweed covered box out of the water. She called out to Simon without looking round.

'You gonna help or what?'

'Right. Yes, of course.'

Simon was painfully aware of how posh his voice sounded compared to hers. He'd been taught to hit all of his T's from an early age. From the sound of things, she'd been taught the opposite.

The very first rock that Simon tried to climb pulled the rug out from under him. With an almighty splash his leg jarred in the icy water between two rocks and he had to crack his forearm against another to save his head from doing it. It took him three attempts to right himself because every time he thought he'd found purchase on one of the rocks it turned icy at the last moment.

He glanced towards Maisie in search of sympathy but she hadn't so much as looked around. In fact, she was already lifting her third box out of the water. Both of Simon's sleeves and trouser legs were soaked through. They weighed down his limbs as he siddled from rock to rock, never standing fully upright, always keeping his arms out wide just in case. A wave jumped up and drenched the rest of him, missing Maisie by inches.

By the time Simon actually knelt down next to her on the rock Maisie had already pulled five of these boxes out of the water. Upon closer inspection he realised they were crab traps, muddy black from seaweed and rot. A couple of them were rattling slightly as their inhabitants scuttled around inside. Maisie stopped Simon just as he reached into the water. He was suddenly aware of how small the rock they were sharing was. Their legs were touching.

'Don't bother.'

'I thought you wanted my help.'

'Yeah, like ten minutes ago when I was pulling these out of the water.'

Simon looked into the swirling grey in front of him.

'There are still traps in there.'

'Oh yeah? Think you can carry 'at many?'

Simon blushed again. Maisie fortunately had turned her back to him, offering the rucksack strapped to her shoulders.

'There's a bucket in there. Get some sea water in it while I crack these open.'

Simon fumbled the zipper. The bucket took up most of the space in the bag. The sea water that he filled it with was cloudy with sand.

'Here, first one comin' up.'

Suddenly there was a crab on Simon's lap, waving its legs helplessly up at him. He jumped. The crab flew up into the air and arced into the sea with a plop.

'Watch it!'

Maisie punched Simon's shoulder so hard he almost toppled sideways into the sea. She had a lot of power for her size.

'Don't tell me you're scared of crabs.'

Simon rubbed his arm and scooped some new water into the now empty bucket.

'Some warning would be nice next time, okay?'

'Oh, yeah sure. How's this? *Excuse me, sir.*'

Maisie put on an awful attempt at a posh accent.

'Sir. I just wanted to draw to your attention a crab. It is currently en route to your bucket. Expected arrival is…'

She checked an imaginary watch.

'…roughly five seconds from now. Is everything in order for said arrival, sir?'

Simon thrust the bucket her way making sure to spill a healthy amount of water onto her jeans. A crab dropped into it.

'Thank you kindly.'

Maybe he should have stayed at the supermarket. He could only imagine the amount of groveling he would have to do to make Aaron even let him through the front doors now.

Before long the bucket was about half full of crabs, each one trying to climb over the other with some hope of escape. Maisie closed the boxes up, stood, and kicked them back down into the depths.

'Wait, what are you doing? There are more crabs in there.'

But Maisie was already hopping back along the rocks towards the sand. She called back over her shoulder to him.

'Hurry up.'

'Why aren't you taking all of them?'

Maisie stopped and gave her most dramatic sigh yet.

'Do I really have to spell it out for you?'

She waited, looking at him for an answer. Simon thought for a moment. It clicked. He scrambled over the rocks after her, peering nervously up at the cliffs.

***

Simon had never stolen anything in his life. One time as a kid he'd stuffed his pockets full of sweets from the cornershop. He'd been on the verge of walking out when the man behind the till smiled at him. Little Simon had burst into tears on the spot, thrown the sweets all over the floor and begged the man not to call the police.

At least this time around he wasn't in tears yet. The bucket of crabs felt heavy in his hand. His eyes raked back and forth over the countryside as the two wound their way along the footpath back into town. Maisie was striding away from him so fast that he had to break into the occasional jog so as not to lose her completely.

'Look, I'm not sure about this.'

Maisie didn't turn back to him so he decided to push on.

'Maisie, I'm not a thief. I don't…'

She whirled round to face him, hair whipping in all directions.

'Oh I'm sorry, Mr Moral Compass. I thought you *wanted* to help me. What was it you said yesterday? Because I'm pretty sure you were begging to follow me around.'

'I'm not following you, I'm…'

'Helping? Wait wait wait, were you actually gonna say helping? What have you done to help me so far? It's not a trick question. Let's have a recap shall we? I got all of the traps out the water. I lifted out all the crabs. I dropped them all in the bucket. Now, what have *you* done? Let's see. You put some water in the bucket. And… that's funny, I can't thinka shit else.'

'I mean, I'm carrying the bucket right now.'

Maisie scowled, turned round and kept walking.

'I don't need you coming into my life telling me what I'm doing is wrong, got it?'

'I'm sorry.'

'God, you're such a wet blanket.'

'What? I apologised, didn't I?'

'You give up *so* easily.'

'Right.'

Their conversation died off as they got back into town. Maisie was making a beeline for the pub. Simon noticed a few broken bottles strewn around on the floor outside. The sign above the door said closed but Maisie pushed it open anyway. Simon glanced up the road towards Aunt Bella and Uncle Aled's cottage. If one of them came out now he wasn't sure he'd have a good enough excuse.

'Earth to dickhead, you coming in or not?'

'Right, yeah. Of course.'

Simon caught his foot as he tried to walk through the door. Dirty sea water splashed out onto the carpet. It was dark enough inside that hopefully no one would notice. Despite neither of them being very tall, they both had to duck under a couple of beams to get to the bar. A slot machine blinked lazily at them as if they'd just woken it up. Maisie cleared her throat loudly.

Footsteps made the ceiling creak inches above their heads. A gruff voice called out from some other room.

''At you, Maisie?'

'Yup.'

A grunt. An apron appeared in the doorway to the kitchen draped loosely over a perfectly circular belly. A man followed the belly into view.

''ow many today?'

Maisie turned to look at Simon, expecting him to answer the man. Before he could, she snatched the bucket out of his hand, spilling more water on the floor. She peered inside and poked a couple of crabs out of the way.

'Five.'

'Fifteen quid.'

'Twenty.'

'Fifteen.'

Maisie shoved the bucket back into Simon's arms. The water sloshed onto his jumper.

'Twenty or you don't get no crabs at all.'

'Jonesy's coming in an hour with his batch, I'll buy extra off him for cheaper.'

'Eighteen.'

'Sixteen.'

'Deal.'

The fat man's hand swallowed up all of Maisie's hand and wrist as they shook. The bucket landed on the bar with a small slosh. The fat man took it and disappeared into the kitchen. Maisie drummed her fingers in the sudden silence. Simon stuck his hands in his pockets, trying to look nonchalant.

After a moment the man reappeared and handed the bucket back to her. They each nodded and turned to walk in separate directions. Simon trailed after Maisie back out into the street.

***

'Alright you actually need to pull your weight this time.'

'I will.'

'No but seriously, if you ain't gonna help me then I ain't having you follow me round all day.'

'I said I will, alright?'

Both of them were short of breath as they followed the narrow road uphill. Simon was slightly nervous about a car bombing round the corner. The tall hedges on either side meant that they wouldn't see it coming until it was too late.

'How much further is it?'

Maisie didn't answer.

'Okay then, what are we doing?'

Again, nothing.

'Alright then, idiots say nothing.'

'You're such a baby.'

Simon laughed. It was a dumb joke. He couldn't see Maisie's face. As usual, she was striding about four steps ahead of him.

'So are you going to tell me where we're going?'

'Oh my god, you are such a child.'

'How's that childish?'

'Are we there yet? Are we there yet?'

'Bet I'm older than you.'

'Bet you're not.'

'Five pounds?'

'No.'

'Come on, I bet five pounds I'm older than you.'

'I don't gamble.'

'Oh don't be so boring, Maisie... Alright we can bet fake money then if you want.'

'Oh my God, fine. If it'll shut you up. How old are you, then?'

'Na-uh. Whatever age I say, you're going to lie and say you're a year older.'

'I ain't.'

'You absolutely are.'

Maisie's hair rippled as she shook her head. Simon grinned.

'A bet's a bet, Maisie. You go first, how old are you?'

It took her a while to respond. So long that Simon started to think that he'd upset her somehow. She was still refusing to even glance back at him. Her hands were clenching and unclenching into little fists.

'Eighteen. My birthday's...'

'Ha! Nineteen. I knew it, you owe me five imaginary quid.'

Maisie didn't reply.

'Oh come on, you're not a sore loser are you?'

She kept walking.

'Maisie?'

But they'd arrived at the house.

An old lady was stood outside waving at them excitedly. She couldn't have been more than five foot in her prime but her old age had hunched her down even lower. A gummy smile lit up her face as she peered at Simon over a thick pair of glasses. She was the lady who'd been winking at him in yoga.

'I see you've brought a friend.'

'Friend's a strong word.'

'Well he's very handsome.'

'He's all yours if you want him.'

The old lady took Simon's hand in both her own bony ones and pulled him in for a closer inspection. Maisie disappeared through the open door into the cottage.

'You remind me of my late husband.'

'Uh thank you, my name's Simon.'

'My goodness you're slim.'

'Well it's not for a lack of trying.'

Inside the cottage there was a clattering sound and the first half of a swear word before Maisie managed to censor herself. The little old lady holding Simon's hand didn't bat an eyelid.

'I'm so sorry, I don't actually know your name?'

'Penelope but my friends call me Penny.'

'It's a lovely name.'

'Careful you, I'm old enough to be your grandmother.'

Simon laughed. He tried to slide his hands out of hers but her grip was surprisingly tight.

'I should probably go in and help Maisie.'

'Nonsense! She can handle it on her own. Besides you need to keep me company.'

'Well, it's just that I said I'd help.'

Penny shushed him and relinquished one of her hands to place a finger on Simon's lips. He tried again to tug his hand free but her grip had tightened.

Maisie was still knocking things over inside. The finger on his mouth smelled stale.

'You couldn't leave little old me out here on my own could you?'

'I really should be heading in.'

'But we're just getting to know each other.'

Simon couldn't be sure because he looked away at just the wrong moment but he was pretty sure she winked at him again. Penny was standing uncomfortably close. She leaned in towards him, her warm breath tickling his chin. It smelled rotten. She was on the verge of saying something when Maisie appeared in the doorway.

Slightly taken aback by the scene in front her, Maisie paused. When she did interrupt, there was a cautious friendliness in her voice that Simon hadn't heard before.

'Hey Simon, could you come and give me a hand with this stuff?'

Penny's grip tightened so much that Simon had to stop himself crying out.

'I was just having a little chat with Simon, he can come in very soon.'

'No.'

Maisie sounded firm, almost aggressive suddenly.

'No, Simon needs to come inside and help me. Now.'

Nobody did anything. Maisie stood in the doorway breathing slightly more heavily than usual. Penny stared at her, Simon still in her clutches. But then the moment was over. Simon was free and the smiling old lady turned back to him and ushered the pair of them inside.

Maisie grabbed Simon's arm as soon as he was through the door and led him upstairs. While the house looked pristine, it smelled otherwise. Simon could just about make out small dark bruises of mould on the walls where the wallpaper curled off in the corners. Penny didn't follow them upstairs.

On the landing, there was a mountain of stuff. The cornerstone of the pile was an ornate trunk, large enough to hold a body. Rising out of it were piles of ornaments, furniture, trinkets and textiles. The mound twinkled at Simon, there were spots of gold and jewels strewn carelessly throughout. Maisie grabbed a bedside lamp and what must have been a jewellery box from the top of the pile.

'You take the heavy stuff.'

'Where are we taking it?'

'Oh you're not gonna like it.'

***

Maisie was right. Simon didn't like it. The entire mountain of stuff had to make its way off Penny's landing, down the flight of stairs, through the front garden, down the lane, out onto the road, down the hill, round the corner and into an old garage. The garage belonged to what looked like an empty house. Maisie extracted the world's most ineffective hairpin from her head to crack the lock. A couple of rats scurried out when they first got it open.

The pair of them spent most of the day going to and fro with various cutlery sets, chests of drawers and old records. Maisie was surprisingly strong for her size and Simon was about as weak as he looked. They both worked up a sweat as the sun rose overhead. Simon's calves burned as he walked all the way back up the hill for what felt like the hundredth time. He'd taken his jumper off at one point but Penny had appeared in a doorway, staring hungrily at his arms, so he quickly threw it back on.

'Is she always like this?'

Maisie took a while to answer. They were both pretty short of breath so neither had been talking much.

'It's my fault.'

'What's your fault?'

But Maisie didn't have time to answer. They were back at the house and had the just the trunk left to carry down the hill. Penny was pottering around in the kitchen. Maisie told Simon to wait upstairs while she sorted out payment. They'd carry this last thing down the hill and not come back up. Simon could hear their muffled voices coming through the floorboards. While he couldn't pick up on the words, he caught Maisie's firm tone from before again. Then she appeared at the top of the stairs, gave Simon a quick grimace and they bent in unison to carry the trunk down the stairs and out.

'Fuck me, this is heavy. Can we stop at the corner?'

Simon agreed and they set it down, just out of view of the house. Simon was just about to press Maisie for answers when she started talking. She spoke fast without looking at him.

'Her husband died three years ago. He was twenty years younger than her. Fell down the stairs apparently. Before him, she had two other husbands. The stuff we've been clearing is mostly theirs.'

Simon shifted on his feet.

'There's always talk around town… you know how it is. You hear things but you don't really think about them. Or just laugh them off. Which, you know. You shouldn't. But sometimes you do anyway. Um, not nice things, you know? I mean, you saw how she was with you. And I'm sorry, if I'd known she'd be so… yeah. If I'd known, I wouldn't have brought you. Or I'd've warned you or something.'

'It's fine, don't worry. I wanted to be here to help, remember?'

'I know. Just sometimes, old men round here can be like that with girls and… just because it's the other way round doesn't mean… it's just not nice. So yeah. Let's just get this to the garage.'

'Sure.'

***

By the time the last of stuff was in the garage it had gone three o'clock. Simon felt slightly dizzy looking at it all. They hadn't had lunch yet. Now that they'd finally stopped working Simon could feel his stomach catching up with him. Maisie suggested they get fish and chips down by the shore. Simon wanted to eat inside but Maisie carried her styrofoam box out of the door and found a spot on the sand. Simon sat a couple of feet away.

They barely spoke as they ate, both of them too hungry to think about much else. Above them stretched one endless cloud. It looked as if God had woken up in the morning and decided that the sky was white now instead of blue. Simon watched Maisie as she speared her last soggy chip.

'You're not from round here either, are you?'

'What gave it away?'

'*What gave it away?*'

Simon tried to imitate her accent but even he could hear how bad of an impression it was. Maisie laughed and had to cover her mouth to stop the chip escaping. She didn't laugh like the girls in movies.

'Can you do us a favour? *Never* do that again.'

'Oh, I fully regret it, don't worry.'

Maisie's smile faded. She closed her styrofoam box and put a rock on it to save it from blowing away. When she looked out across the ocean the wind blew the hair over her face, hiding it from Simon.

'You didn't answer my question. You know I'm from London, staying with my aunt and uncle. But what about you? Why are you here?'

'Mmm, that's the question innit. Why oh why.'

'Do you want to leave too?'

Maisie took her time before answering.

'I guess I want change. I don't like how things are. And I want them to be different.'

'Nice dodge.'

'Look, can we just enjoy this? Like right now. Without getting all deep or anything.'

'Yeah, sure. That's fine.'

But when Simon looked out over the ocean things didn't feel all that fine for some reason. The girl sat two feet away from him was just as mysterious as the day she'd flipped him off at the beach.

Maisie shuffled a couple of inches towards him. Simon grinned.

'Careful, people might think we're actually friends.'

He'd put his foot in it. He could tell straight away. Maisie sat still for a moment before snatching up her empty box and storming off back towards town.

'Maisie?'

But she'd already hopped over the sea wall and disappeared, hair billowing in the wind.

***

Simon still had a couple of hours to kill before he could head home. He wasn't looking forward to lying to his uncle. For some reason he didn't feel so bad lying to Aunt Bella.

He found his usual spot up on the coastal path and sat on the rock. The jumper was still hanging from the fencepost. The grass under him was slightly damp but he was beyond caring. Most of his clothes were soaked in sweat at this point anyway. Glancing over his shoulder he could just about make out Penny's house poking out over the crest of the hill. He shivered and looked back out to sea instead.

Maisie hadn't paid him. They hadn't talked about tomorrow either. For all Simon knew, he'd just been fired. Funnily enough, he didn't actually care too much about either of those things. He definitely wasn't upset about hurting her feelings either.

To be honest, she was starting to piss him off. He was nice to her. He was helping her. Sure he got things wrong, but that's because she never told him what the hell they were doing. How was he supposed to know what to do or what to say? She never gave him any answers. Then he'd say something harmless and she'd start sulking.

But as Simon sat there watching the sea knitting tiny little foamy lines, that would glide up the sand before being pulled back in, he felt the anger starting to ebb out of him.

The walkie-talkie was heavy in his pocket. Simon fished it out and toyed with the button for a while before finally pressing it down.

'Hey, um. It's me. Simon. I don't know if these even work. Um, you might not have it turned on or something. Anyway, I just wanted to say that I, uh, I enjoyed today. Not the bit with the creepy old lady. Or the bit where I fell in the sea. But the rest of it was alright. I was just wondering if you'd be happy for me to join you again on Monday? I can meet you in the same place again? Yeah. So, yeah. I'm sorry as well. For what I said. I uh, yeah. I'm sorry. See you at church?'

Simon's heart was hammering when he let go of the button. He debated saying something else but decided against it. He sat there for an hour with the walkie-talkie perched on the rock beside him, watching the sea repeat itself, again and again.

***

Simon got straight into the shower when he got home before Aunt Bella could get to him. He kept the walkie-talkie on the sink as he did. It was back in his pocket as they ate dinner together. With the taste of fish and chips still in his mouth, Simon struggled to get through half of the stuff on his plate. Aunt Bella didn't push him to eat more this evening.

As Simon lay in bed staring at the ceiling he wondered for what felt like the thousandth time how long he would be here. How many more half-eaten meals were there between him and his home? How many more nights staring at this same view? How many more times would he see-

The walkie-talkie crackled. Simon jumped. The little red light on it lit up his room. For a while there was just white noise. What if Aunt Bella heard? Simon twisted the knob on the top and turned it right down just as the walkie-talkie whispered into his ear.

'Don't be late.'

***

By the time Sunday came around Simon remembered why he'd wanted a job so much in the first place. All Saturday Aunt Bella had been taking him from one place to the next: garden shops, a second hand auction, three different rug shops and, in the evening the eighty fifth birthday party of a lady from church. Simon knew he must have spoken to her at some point but a lot of the faces from church blended together into one wrinkly smiling blob.

Aunt Bella was clearly a woman of tradition though. Sundays were rest days. And Simon needed one of them. It had only been a few days since he'd flown off the bike and all of the aches had come back with a vengeance after his day helping Maisie.

Simon had been thinking it over a lot. He had a lot of time to think now that his phone was busted and he'd spent most of his day hanging out with his aunt and uncle. The way he saw it, Maisie wasn't doing anything *that* wrong. They'd stolen crabs in the morning *but* the crabs were still technically in the sea. That kind of made them fair game. Besides they'd taken fewer than half of them.

With clearing Penny's house, that was an easy one. They'd been paid to throw out all the stuff. All they were doing was making a bit of profit selling it on, that was all. Nothing wrong there. If anything they were doing a good thing because they were stopping it from ending up in some landfill site. Also, Simon struggled to feel all that bad for Penny.

That said, he did still give a quick apology to the man upstairs as he took his pew. As usual he'd taken the spot at the front with Aunt Bella and Uncle Aled. He had to keep up appearances that he wasn't spending time with Maisie. They'd be suspicious enough already since he didn't come home in his uniform on Friday.

Simon resisted the urge to look back until the first hymn. Sure enough, rising up from the back cutting clearly through all of the pensioners in between came Maisie's voice. It was his third Sunday hearing that voice and it still made him shiver slightly. Annoying as she was, Maisie sure could sing.

As part of the sermon the vicar asked them all to think about their friendships. More specifically, to shout out the things that they thought made a good friendship. Simon kept his mouth shut.

'You trust them with your life.'

He barely trusted her with his walkie-talkie.

'They're always there for you.'

Nope.

'Good friendships are the ones where you're completely open with each other.'

'Yeah, no secrets.'

As if.

So that was that. Maisie wasn't his friend. That was clear enough. Work colleague? Sure, he'd go with that. That was, if she was happy with him keeping his job. Tomorrow he'd be better. Definitely. He hadn't been all that bad before. Sure he didn't help much with the crabs but he did a good job carrying the stuff around with her. If that was all he was needed for, then it couldn't be too bad.

She must've had other projects too. Her wallet *had* looked pretty full in the supermarket. It must have all come from somewhere. Simon felt a familiar uneasiness in his stomach. He'd said he didn't care about the law but now that he was in church he wasn't so sure.

Round and round Simon's thoughts went until suddenly the service was over. All of the little old people were tottering over to the back of the hall to get their teas and biscuits. Simon caught a flash of a lurid knitted jumper as it disappeared out of the door.

'Hey Aunt Bella, I'm just going to get some air quickly.'

'Sweetie, are you feeling okay? Are you sure that you haven't got a concussion? Is there something you haven't been telling…'

But Simon was already disappearing through the elderly throng.

'Maisie, wait up. Maisie.'

He managed to catch her just around the corner. Thankfully, out of view from the front doors. Maisie was slow to turn around.

'Listen, I just wanted to say- Oh god.'

Maisie's lip was swollen. A recently reopened cut was oozing blood slightly. She licked it away and looked at the floor.

'What happened? Are you okay?'

'I'm fine, what did you want to say?'

'I, uh, I just wanted to say sorry. Listen Maisie, what's happening? You turned up last week with a black eye and now this.'

'I don't want to talk about it.'

'Is someone hurting you?'

'Why do you care?'

'Because…'

Yeah, he'd say it.

'Because you're my friend.'

The corner of her mouth might have twitched for a moment, he couldn't tell. Her eyes were still looking at the floor. She was tugging at a loose thread on one of her sleeves.

'I'll tell you tomorrow, okay?'

'Okay.'

'Don't be late.'

And Maisie turned around and walked away. He wasn't quite sure but it looked like her head was held a bit higher than usual this time.

Chapter 7

He had to be more careful. He was kicking himself for it really. When Simon had turned around to go back into church Aunt Bella had been there behind him on the road, eyes sharp. She had seen something was up. That evening she'd even asked him why he'd wanted the other walkie-talkie back and who he'd given it too. He hadn't technically been lying when he said someone at work but it didn't make him feel less guilty.

'Don't worry about her. She's...'

But Aunt Bella had never finished that sentence. The words echoed round Simon's head as he stood on that exact same spot on the beach where he'd heard them before. The morning was crisp. The wind was blowing hard as ever. The sun was up earlier than usual, his only company as he waited for Maisie to arrive.

When the tangle of hair and ugly jumper appeared on the coastal path, Simon almost caught himself smiling.

Maisie's lip had scabbed over. The black eye she'd been sporting before had mostly gone too. As she walked towards him he was struck once again by her size. She wouldn't pose a threat to anyone and yet here she was with war wounds written across her face.

He'd taken a bucket from home and stored it away in his bag. The dramatic reveal that he'd planned didn't really have the impact he wanted as he held it out and called out to her.

'Crabs?'

Maisie rolled her eyes but a little smile played on her lips too. Wordlessly they wandered over to the water's edge and let the waves gently lick at their shoes, waiting. The sea was reserved. It was watching them to see what would happen next. Simon waited for Maisie to break the silence. Eventually she did.

'There's a car boot sale going on at the primary school today. The one opposite the supermarket. S'not far from where we stored Penny's crap. We'll get the crabs then start moving stuff over there.'

'Sounds good.'

'We can sort the money after.'

'Cool.'

'Oh and uh, nice try with the second bucket. Can't use it though.'

'Why's that?'

'We can only steal so many crabs before it looks suspicious.'

'I thought about that, don't worry.'

Maisie turned to him. It felt good being the one in the know for once. Simon pointed to the rock pool on the other the end of the beach.

'No one crabs over there.'

'Yeah, because they're all the shit little ones that get washed away.'

'Exactly. We catch some from that side, carry them across to the traps and replace the crabs we take with the smaller ones. That way we can take more.'

'Huh.'

Out of the corner of his eye Simon could see Maisie nodding. He tried to fight back a smile but lost.

'Alright, let's try it.'

'Maybe I'm not completely useless after all.'

'Sure.'

So they split up. Simon went to one end of the beach to catch some small crabs, Maisie to the other to get the traps. Simon's balance was much better on this side of the beach. The rocks were smooth but flatter. Scurrying around in the gaps between them under a few inches of water were a dozen or so tiny crabs. They pinched at his fingers as he tried to pick them out and into his bucket but they were too small to do any real damage.

Maisie joined him before he was done. She was still much better at this than he was. Kneeling down next to him, not caring about getting damp knees, she helped him pick out the last ones and they walked the bucket across the beach together to where the traps lay patiently waiting.

'Alright, fine. This was a good idea.'

'How many crabs did you get?'

'Ten.'

'Not bad.'

'Not bad at all.'

***

Maisie only stopped to count the money from the pub once they opened the garage door. She perched herself on a little pile of doilies and flipped through the notes one by one. There were only four of them, two tens and five as per her request, but she smiled at them nonetheless. Simon watched her with a little bubble of pride growing in his chest. Very carefully, Maisie separated the notes into two fifteens and put one in her pocket. The other one she held out to him.

'I'll give you Friday's money once we sell all this stuff. It'll be easier to split it all once than split some now and some later.'

'Sure.'

Fifteen pounds. It wasn't much to anyone but Simon carefully folded it and tucked it away as if it were priceless. Maisie was watching him.

'You know, I don't make as much money as you think. Like, my wallet when you saw in the supermarket. I've been saving that for a while. And... I have to give a lot of it away.'

'Okay.'

'I'm just saying, you won't get rich working with me.'

'Okay.'

'You can always go back...'

'To the supermarket?'

'Yeah.'

Simon laughed. He put his hand on her shoulder.

'Maisie, no amount of money is making me set foot in that supermarket again.'

'You sure?'

'You're not getting rid of me that easily.'

Maisie smiled. Suddenly, the hand on her shoulder felt a bit awkward. Simon shoved it into his pocket instead.

'So uh, what should we carry across first?'

***

Everything felt lighter today. All of the furniture that had threatened to snap Simon's fingers on Friday now felt manageable. He chatted with Maisie as they carried stuff across, mostly about nothing: their old high schools, the weather, a lady who walked by with a dog in a pushchair. Maisie was surprisingly easy to talk to when she wasn't in a huff.

'So what's the master plan when you get back to London?'

'Honestly, I don't know. I think I'll just appreciate everything more. Friends, my bed, the city, you don't realise how much you like this stuff until it's gone.'

Maisie nodded knowingly. Simon decided to press his luck.

'You never actually told me how you ended up here.'

'My dad.'

'You live with him?'

'Mhm. Just me and him. Few years ago someone promised him a job out here building sea walls. And well, you don't see many sea walls round here, do you?'

'And you never moved back?'

'Couldn't afford it, not with dad's…'

But Maisie stopped herself. There was the line. Neither of them spoke for a minute. Simon figured it was only fair he opened up to her a bit as well.

'I miss my mum most. Aunt Bella's lovely, she really is, but she's a bit… I don't know, intense? She likes to treat me like her little boy.'

'Does she have kids?'

'She did. He lived around here. Huw? Might've died before you came here. He, uh, he had some problems that he never quite got over.'

Maisie nodded. They put down the chest of drawers in the field. They'd been so wrapped up in conversation they hadn't noticed the school field filling up with cars and people holding boxes of things to sell.

'I didn't really know him that much. I was younger then and I don't think my parents really wanted me to see him in his state. He drank a lot.'

'My dad drinks.'

Maisie's voice was quiet. So quiet that Simon barely heard her. Slowly, as they walked back to get more stuff, the scars and bruises on her face started to make sense to Simon.

***

This was probably the first day Simon could remember in Wales that didn't drag by. He and Maisie worked their stall instinctively. Maisie would stride back and forth in front of their wares calling out to people, singing songs and generally drawing attention their way. All the while Simon would smile at any passersby and make up obscure facts about the things they were selling.

Their prices were higher than anyone else's, something which Simon proposed and Maisie was hesitant about. He'd told her that everyone here was retired. That meant surprisingly deep pockets for doilies, trinkets, and lampshades. Just like the crabs in the morning, he'd been right again. As Maisie sung the praises of their premium goods, freshly acquired antiques from a supposedly large estate, Simon would ask people how their days were going, talk about how lovely the weather was and how thrifty their prices actually were.

He did have to keep an eye out though. Whenever anyone from church would show up he'd duck down behind the chest of drawers and count the money to avoid being seen. If anyone saw him here it would undoubtedly make its way back to Aunt Bella. Or worse yet, what if Aunt Bella showed up today? He'd managed to just about pull the wool over her eyes about Maisie once. He didn't fancy his chances of doing it again.

Maisie appeared at his side and elbowed his ribs.

'Goin' alright, innit?'

'Yeah, I'm surprised. People really want to buy this rubbish.'

'Higher – sorry – *premium* prices, huh? You've got a bigger brain than you let on, Simon.'

'Thanks. You're not a bad saleswoman yourself.'

'You think so?'

'Yeah, of course.'

Maisie grinned and rocked from side to side a bit. When she spoke it was in a very careful precise voice.

'You know, it's always been a dream of mine.'

'What has? Selling stuff?'

'Yeah, like I reckon I could be pretty good.'

'What would you sell?'

Maisie gestured shyly at her torso.

'Your body?'

'A better woman than me would slap you for that. No, you dickhead. My jumpers.'

She pulled at the hem of her lurid knitted jumper.

'Oh, *you* make those?'

'Mhm.'

'I never realised.'

'You don't like 'em.'

'I never said that.'

'You didn't deny it either.'

'Do *you* like them?'

'Course I do, I made 'em.'

'Well then they're fine by me.'

Maisie smiled at him and started to wander back into her sales battle station.

'One day, I'll sell 'em.'

'And I can be the dickhead who follows you around carrying the bucket.'

Maisie laughed.

'I'm holding you to that.'

Then she was singing again at the top of her voice to the little old ladies walking past. They came over and bought a coat rack for £20. One of them even pinched Simon's cheek before leaving.

'If we keep making money at this rate I'll be off to London by Friday.'

Maisie was about to reply when she stopped dead. Her eyes grew almost comically wide. Simon followed her gaze. Rounding the corner, wrapped up in a coat with a big old handbag, was Aunt Bella.

Simon dropped to the grass just in time. Maisie wasn't so lucky. Simon saw her legs stiffen. She'd been spotted. His eyes clawed across the field, looking for somewhere, anywhere, to hide. Nothing. Nothing he could get to at least. Maisie kicked him. He looked up. She was nudging her thumb to the right. He crawled in that direction and rounded the corner of the chest of draws just as he heard Aunt Bella's voice right next to where he'd just been.

'Good afternoon.'

'Alright?'

Maisie sounded calm as anything. If Aunt Bella decided to peer around the corner of the drawers he was finished.

'Anything you'd like to buy? We've sold quite a lot already but there's still some good stuff here.'

'Yes, I can see.'

Aunt Bella's voice had an edge to it. One that Simon hadn't heard before.

'And may I ask, sweetie, where is all of this from?'

'Everything you see here is locally sourced. All antique, all high quality.'

'Is it indeed?'

'It is.'

'So is any of it your own?'

'Well, I *am* selling it.'

'Sweetie, that isn't what I asked.'

'What are you suggesting?'

'Oh nothing dear, I just like to buy things that are ethically sourced.'

Simon heard Maisie shifting her weight.

'Can I interest you in a new jewellery box?'

'No, sweetie. No you cannot.'

'Well, I hope you find something you like from someone else then.'

Simon let out a sigh as he heard Aunt Bella walking away. He was about to get into a more comfortable position when she stopped.

'Simon's a good lad. You stay away from him. If he found out what you did…'

'Don't worry. I won't corrupt your perfect little nephew.'

Maisie's voice had taken on the same edge. This time Aunt Bella left for good. Simon stayed crouched behind the chest of drawers waiting for Maisie to call him out.

'Alright, she's gone.'

'You sure?'

'Mhm.'

Simon got up and brushed himself off.

'That was *way* too close. If she'd seen me…'

Maisie wasn't listening though. Her fingers were fiddling with her sleeve again. Her eyes were glancing around the field.

'Maisie, are you alright?'

'Hm? Yeah, yeah. I'm top, don't worry.'

'You don't look like it.'

She flashed him a token smile.

'Let's just sell the rest of this.'

'Sure… Maisie, you do know that I'm cool hanging out with you, right? Aunt Bella doesn't scare me.'

'She's got a point though. There's some stuff you don't know.'

'You might not've noticed but there's a lot of stuff I don't know. I'm getting pretty used to it at this point.'

'You sure?'

'Certain. Now let's sell the rest of this junk and go home.'

Simon gave her shoulder a little squeeze. Maisie didn't look at him but a small smile danced across her lips. Her curly hair caught the breeze and started dancing softly. Simon watched it sway this way and that until the breeze died down, revealing Aunt Bella standing behind her, mouth agape.

***

'Simon, this doesn't help your case at all.'

'Look, I know. Okay?'

'But that's not good enough, honey. You always say the same thing. When you'd get in trouble at school, when you'd laze around at home all day, when I'd have to tell you off for anything. Ever since you were a little boy. I know, mum. I'm sorry, mum. If you know you're doing something wrong then why do you do it? Hm?'

'Mum, it's not as bad as it sounds.'

'Is it not? Really? You've lied to your aunt and uncle. You've lied to me. You quit your job without telling us.'

'I know.'

'Stop saying you know!'

The phone went quiet. Simon waited for his mum to continue.

'Simon, I need you to answer me truthfully here. Aunt Bella says you've been stealing. Is that true?'

'We didn't steal any of the stuff we were selling.'

'Then where did it all come from?'

'A lady from up the hill asked us to clear the junk out of her house. We were just selling it on.'

'Did she ask you to sell it?'

'Well, no.'

'Then it wasn't yours to sell.'

'Mum, can we not have this argument?'

'If you didn't want this argument then you shouldn't have done all of this in the first place.'

'I know.'

'Simon!'

'Can I tell my side? Am I allowed to do that? Because since I've come to this f- this town, everyone's been speaking for me. It's like no one around here cares what *I* have to say.'

Simon knew Aunt Bella was listening from the next room. Screw it, she could do with hearing this too.

'My job at the supermarket sucked, okay? The manager was a twat, my coworkers were zombies, I worked till I literally bled, I crashed the bike on the way home, it… it sucked, okay? Would you have wanted me to work there for a month then come home? What lesson would that teach me? Is that what constitutes being an adult? Getting screwed over at your job long enough to save up enough money to buy something new? If that's what being an adult is then maybe I don't want to grow up.'

'Simon, honey. Not everything you do in life is going to be fun.'

'You're not listening.'

'Simon, I'm happy for you to get another job but this Maisie girl, she's bad news.'

'Oh and you know that, do you? From all the way back home in London you can tell?'

'I've heard things from your aunt.'

'She's the only person in this town who's actually doing anything. Everyone else here is either working a shit job or waiting to die.'

'*Simon*. I will not have you using that kind of language with me.'

'Maisie's not a bad person.'

'Your aunt and I don't think you should be spending time with her.'

'And what does Uncle Aled think? Hm? No one ever asks him how he feels either.'

'I'm sure he feels the same way as your aunt and I.'

'Oh are you now? Just like you were sure that I had a lovely job at the supermarket? Just like you're sure that Maisie's a bad person.'

'Simon.'

'Look, I'm going to keep working with her whether you and Aunt Bella like it or not. I'm gonna prove you wrong about her.'

'And what work is that exactly? Stealing?'

'No. We're… we're selling jumpers.'

'Selling jumpers.'

'Yeah.'

'And whose idea was this?'

'Maisie's.'

'And how many jumpers have you sold?'

'None yet.'

'And what exactly do you do to help? Knitting?'

'Business, er, strategy.'

'Business strategy. Right.'

'Look I'm trying my best here, okay? Maybe we won't ever sell a single jumper. Maybe I'll have to go back to being miserable stacking shelves for the rest of my life. But let me try. I know you and Aunt Bella don't like Maisie. I know that neither of you believe in me but I'm gonna try my best to prove you both wrong. Alright? And if I mess it up then I mess it up. You can say 'I told you so' then. You can laugh at me all you want but let me give this a go first. I'm not gonna give and get a shit job yet.'

The line was silent for so long that Simon thought his mum must have hung up. He'd just taken the phone away from his ear to put it down when she spoke.

'I don't want you to be miserable. If you really believe in this Maisie girl then it's up to you. I just don't want to see you get hurt, honey.'

'I'm sorry for swearing.'

'And I'm sorry for shouting. I love you.'

'I love you too, mum.'

'Okay.'

Simon waited by the phone for a while after he hung up. Aunt Bella and Uncle Aled were in the dining room with dinner on the table. He could smell the gravy. As much as his stomach growled for it he couldn't bring himself to speak to them. He'd never seen Aunt Bella as furious as she'd been earlier. He'd been able to talk his mum down, he wasn't sure he could do the same with his aunt.

Quietly as he could, Simon padded upstairs to his room. The stairs creaked a little as he scaled them but he didn't care that much about being heard. He just hoped they weren't waiting for him to join them at the table before they ate. His room didn't feel like his own anymore. All of the pictures of Huw on the walls were watching him. The bed had been bought for someone else.

There were a million and one different ways that he could see his conversation with Aunt Bella going. Simon lay on his back, staring at the ceiling, playing them all out in his head. The light flooding through his window stretched and dimmed until it was barely any different from the shadows on the ceiling. His stomach stopped aching after a while. It got used to being empty.

***

The knock at the door pulled Simon out of the shallow end of sleep.

It took him a moment to organise what had been a dream, what he'd been imagining, and what had actually happened. He wasn't in a fit state to argue with Aunt Bella now. She probably knew it, that was why she'd waiting until he'd dozed off to come and argue. He supposed he couldn't put this off any longer.

'Come in.'

But when the door opened, it wasn't Aunt Bella who came in. It was Uncle Aled carrying a tea tray with a steaming bowl of food.

'Hungry?'

Simon smiled weakly and took the tray from his uncle. For the first couple of mouthfuls he tried to act nonchalant but quickly gave up and stuffed his face. The bed creaked softly as his uncle sat down next to him. Simon finished eating in silence. He scooped up the last of the gravy as well as he could with his fork before setting his cutlery down. Uncle Aled was looking at the pictures of Huw on the wall.

'I'm, um... I'm sorry for everything. I shouldn't have lied. I shouldn't have shouted at mum. I'll tell Aunt Bella I'm sorry too.'

Uncle Aled got up from the bed. He took the tray of food from Simon, neatly arranging the knife and fork so they wouldn't fall, and walked over to the open door. The clock on the wall told him it was midnight. The lights were still on in the hallway. Uncle Aled stopped in the doorway and turned back to Simon. His brow was furrowed. Then his face softened as he decided the words he wanted to say. A smile played on his lips.

'I catch fish. You sell jumpers.'

Simon grinned. His uncle grinned back. It was the face of a man half his age that shone through. He started to laugh as he stood in the doorway. It was a sound that poured colour back into the house as he carried the tray back downstairs.

Simon sat on his bed for a long time.

***

It was late when Simon picked up the walkie-talkie from his bedside table. He hesitated before pressing the button to talk to Maisie. She'd probably be asleep. He did it anyway.

'Maisie. It's me. Simon.'

No reply.

'About today, I just wanted you to know it doesn't change anything. I'll still be there tomorrow morning if you are?'

The walkie-talkie crackled.

'What about your aunt? Isn't she pissed?'

'I mean, yeah. Yeah, she was pretty pissed. So was mum when she found out.'

'And you still want to come?'

'Mhm.'

'Do you ever think, you know, maybe you shouldn't?'

'What?'

'Well, what if they're right? About me. You're a good person and I'm... well, I'm me.'

'Oh I'm not nearly as good as you think.'

'Really?'

'Yeah, one time I didn't thank the driver when I got off the bus.'

'No way.'

'Another time, there was this sign that said 'Don't walk on the grass'.'

'And you walked on it?'

'I ran on it.'

'You did not.'

'Sometimes I even ask for takeaway when I know I'll be eating in.'

Simon could hear her giggling. He wondered where she was right now, what her bedroom looked like, whether she was looking at the same view he was. Or maybe she was sat in front of the TV. Or leaning on the counter in her kitchen having a midnight snack.

'Maisie, there's something I want to talk to you about.'

'Yeah? Shoot.'

'Not now. Tomorrow.'

'What is it a surprise or something?'

'No. Well, kind of. Listen, I've got to go and look a few things up but I'll explain it all tomorrow.'

'Uh sure, okay. I don't think we'll have much on tomorrow anyway.'

'Perfect.'

'You gonna tell me what it is?'

'You'll have to wait and see.'

'God, you're a dickhead.'

'Sleep tight.'

***

The computer downstairs took even longer to turn on than Simon remembered. It was so loud that he was worried his aunt or uncle would come in at any moment to ask what he was doing up at this time. With a cup of tea in one hand and the mouse in the other he started his research. There was a pen and notepad next to him, the ones he'd got on his first day at the supermarket.

As the night crawled by the pages filled up with sums, notes and little drawings. Simon worked by the bluish glow of the screen, stopping only to yawn and stretch occasionally. Every sum he checked, double checked and triple checked, afraid that his sleep deprived brain would get something wrong but by the time he finished his work he was confident in the number scrawled at the bottom of the page. So confident that he underlined it three times and circled it twice.

The clock on the wall told him it was approaching 5:30. If he got into bed now he could probably catch about an hour's sleep. He couldn't see it happening though. His brain had passed the point of sleep a couple of hours ago and was now raring for the next day. He could go and shower now and get started with the day. Better yet, he could make a fry up for his sleeping aunt and uncle.

Simon flipped the notepad shut and put it in his pocket before going into the kitchen in the hunt for bacon. It wasn't long before a sizzling sound filled the room and the salty smell of bacon wafted throughout the house. Even the sun peered through the window at the smell.

Chapter 8

'Well you look awful.'

'Good morning to you too.'

'Did you sleep at all last night?'

'Nope.'

'Well?

'Well what?

'You gonna spill the beans on this big secret or not?'

'I don't know what you're talking about.'

'Ah come on, you dickhead. I hate surprises.'

'Oh well in that case, I'll wait till we've got the crabs in first.'

'Are you serious?'

'Yeah, come on. The crabs won't liberate themselves.'

'I actually hate you. This better be worth it.'

Simon just tapped his nose knowingly. Making breakfast had woken him back up even if the bags under his eyes said otherwise. He'd wanted to leave it all laid out on the table and sneak out but Aunt Bella had appeared in the doorway just as the toast popped. They didn't talk about the previous day at all. They didn't talk about anything really but she did give him a hug. Just as Simon had left Uncle Aled had appeared on the stairs wearing an encouraging smile.

For the first time the cold seawater actually felt pretty good as it splashed up at him from between the rocks. There were fewer little crabs scuttling around this morning but he still managed to pinch a few into his bucket before Maisie appeared at his shoulder. How she managed to fill her bucket so quickly every time he would never know.

'So what is it?'

'What's what?'

'Oh my God, can you just tell me? Please?'

Simon laughed. Honestly, he was as excited to tell Maisie as she was frustrated with waiting.

'Alright, alright. I'll tell you.'

Maisie dropped her bucket into the wet sand and folded her arms expectantly. Simon took his time picking out one last little crab before dropping it into his own bucket and joining her on the sand.

'So, obviously I got in a bit of trouble last night.'

'Mhm.'

'Aunt Bella rang my mum and told her what was happening. Mum, as usual, was pretty pissed so I kind of told her a bit of a lie.'

'What kinda lie?'

'Oh nothing big don't worry.'

Maisie raised her eyebrows.

'I told her that we sell jumpers together.'

Maisie scoffed.

'Obviously it was a lie, right? But it got me thinking, what if it wasn't?'

'What d'you mean?'

'Well you said yesterday your dream is to make and sell jumpers, right? So last night I did all the maths on it and…'

'Hang on, hang on. I wasn't being serious about that stuff. Like, we can't *actually* start selling jumpers.'

'Why not?'

'Because… because we can't.'

'Do you want to sell jumpers?'

'I mean, yeah.'

'Well then hear me out, okay?'

Maisie's brow furrowed and her arms crossed tighter but she didn't say anything. Simon pulled the notepad out of his pocket.

'So, like I was saying, I did some maths last night. I went online and looked up all the costs for everything. Wool, shipping, website stuff, renting a studio, all of it. I had to guess a few things like how long it would take you to knit each jumper and how many you've done already. Basically I just went through and priced out how much it would cost to get a little business started for you.'

'Renting a studio?'

'Only a little one. And round here that stuff's super cheap so don't worry about that. Basically, all told it would cost about £5,362 to get you started.'

'Wait, why d'you do all that?'

'Don't know.'

'No, seriously. That's like, a lot of effort. How long did it take?'

'A few hours.'

'A few *hours*?'

'It's not a big deal.'

'Mate, I... I... Ah! What do you want me to say? Like, you know it's never gonna happen right?'

Simon's stomach dropped a little.

'Why not?'

'Because... I'm me. I'm Maisie, alright? I'm *broke*. I scam old people and steal crabs and shit. My dad takes half the money I make. Do you know how long it would take me to save that much?'

'You've been saving already though.'

'What? The cash in my wallet? Mate, that's only like a grand. If that. And that took *months*.'

Simon put the notepad back in his pocket. He could feel a stone sitting somewhere in his gut. Maybe it wasn't realistic.

'Look, Simon. It's nice that you did that. It really is, I 'ppreciate it. But it's just not gonna happen is it? Where can you get that kind of money round here? We're stealing crabs for like twenty quid.'

'Yeah, no, you're right. I guess I just thought… I don't know. Bit sleep deprived.'

'It's nice to have dreams sometimes…'

Maisie squeezed his arm.

'…but that's all it ever was, okay? It's just not gonna happen and you know what? That's fine. I shouldn't'a said anything in the first place. Just a silly little dream, right? Just my imagination running away is all. Now come on, let's ditch the crabs before we get caught.'

For the first time as they walked up to the pub, Maisie didn't walk ahead of him. She kept perfectly in stride next to Simon all the way into town. Neither of them said much.

***

Maisie had a new scheme planned for today. Or at least, one that was new to Simon. They walked a little route through town, knocking on the occasional door to collect shoppings list and handfuls of cash. Most of the lists were quite small but a couple of the old people handed over sheets of paper that made Simon groan.

Once they had a small stack of shopping lists, and a larger stack of cash, they started the long walk over to Simon's old supermarket. They stopped just around the corner so Maisie could consult the lists before going in.

'Ay, gimme a hand with this.'

Simon took half of the lists from her. She handed him a pen.

'Go through and circle everything that's small enough to fit in my jumper.'

'I'm sorry?'

'The small stuff. Toothpaste, jars, and that. Oh and the expensive stuff too.'

'Why?'

'Why d'you think? You know numbers. If we paid for everything on the list where'd the profit come from? We take the grocery money, pay for the half the stuff, keep the change. Victimless crime.'

Simon opened his mouth to protest but then realised that the only victim of this crime would be Aaron. He closed his mouth.

'Now hurry up and get circling.'

'You know I can't go in too right? Aaron would be on me in a flash.'

'Uh-huh.'

'So what should I do instead?'

'I dunno, stand guard or something.'

'Guard against what? The neighbourhood watch?'

Maisie rolled her eyes. They finished circling the small and expensive items on the lists and Maisie scanned them quickly before nodding to herself. Seemingly satisfied that her jumper could conceal enough she grabbed a trolley from outside the door and gave Simon a quick nod before disappearing through inside.

Simon sighed and sat down on a low brick wall. The notebook was cutting into his leg through his pocket. Maisie was probably right. It had been nice to imagine just for a few hours that they could do something in this town, that there was some kind of opportunity here for them. But no. Of course there wasn't. This was a part of the world where people came to live their last few years in peace, staring out towards the horizon. People didn't come here to start their lives, they came here to have a quiet ending.

In Simon's head he'd been imagining the pair of them at the head of a business empire, making money hand over fist, all because he'd stayed up late one evening looking up the price of wool on the internet. In the real world he was here, sat on a damp brick wall with all the money he had in the world stuffed in his left pocket. Maisie was right. Where could he possibly find the kind of money they'd need?

Just then, the automatic doors squeaked open and from somewhere deep inside the supermarket Simon heard one of the tills opening.

***

'Alright, Maisie just hear me out okay?'

'Nope.'

'Two seconds to let me explain. That's all I need.'

'Nope.'

'Maisie, come on.'

'No. How many times do I have to say it?'

She was walking ahead of him again. They were on the coastal path heading back, three heavy bags of shopping in each hand. There was a jar in one of Simon's bags that kept whacking his shin every few steps he took. Maisie was shaking her head sending ripples through her hair as it whipped at Simon's face.

'Maisie, please.'

'*No.* You're being dumb. Like really dumb, okay?'

'It's not as crazy as it sounds.'

One of her bags split. Pasta, tins, celery and eggs all burst free and scattered in every direction, rolling around in the mud.

'Oh for fuck's sake!'

Simon placed his own bags down and rushed over to help. He put what he could into his own bags but they looked like they were all heading for a similar fate. Maisie was trying to fit a loaf of bread into one of her other bags but managed to tear that one too. She slumped on a rock, head in hands.

'Maisie, it's fine. I've got room in my bags. I can take that stuff.'

'A heist?'

'Maisie...'

'A *heist*? You want to do a heist *here*?'

'I was going for dramatic effect when I said that.'

'Like Ocean's Eleven. Like the Italian Job. *Here*?'

'I mean, we'd only be stealing a few thousand. It's more petty theft really.'

'So it was a heist a minute ago and now it's just petty theft?'

'Look Maisie, all I'm saying is…'

'*No*. We are not robbing the supermarket. What the hell's gotten into you?'

'It's not as crazy as it sounds.'

'The more you say that, the crazier it's sounding!'

'Maisie, there's a safe in the back. I think Aaron's got-'

'Aaron?'

'The manager. Moustache guy. He's got a safe in the back office where he puts all the money he nicks from the tills.'

'Oh okay, so you'll rapel from the ceiling and dust for prints while I prep the getaway car.'

'Maisie.'

'No. This is so dumb. I'm not even gonna think about it. What if we get caught?'

'We'll plan it so we don't.'

'Brilliant, you're a genius! Oh you've cracked. We just won't get caught! I'll call up all the people in prison this side of the Severn and tell 'em where they went wrong.'

'We can figure something out.'

'And what about the people we're stealing from? Huh? What if the supermarket goes bust or people get fired?'

'They won't go bust, we'll be stealing - taking - from the safe. It's already stolen money. And no one's getting fired because they got robbed, that's like arresting someone for getting hit by a car... it's a victimless crime.'

Maisie scowled at him.

'If you quote me back at me again, I'll break your skinny little arms. This is Wales, alright? We're not in like Hatton Gardens or whatever. We're not in Vegas. This isn't an action movie.'

'Exactly. People won't expect it.'

'Simon. People won't expect it because it's dumb as shit. Now shut up and help me carry this stuff.'

'What if-'

'If you say one more word about this heist...'

'Just think of the money, alright? You could be your selling jumpers in time for Christmas. I could have any phone I want and be on the first train out of here. Mum couldn't possibly say I haven't proven myself when I show her a stack of thousands.'

'If you care about money so much, *here*.'

Maisie pulled a fistful of notes out of her pocket and threw them at him. The wind caught them and Simon had to scramble after the twirling paper so it wouldn't fly off the cliff edge into the sea. When he turned back to Maisie, her eyes looked wet. Her voice was almost steady when she spoke.

'There's all of my money from today. If you wanna get out of here so bad then take it. Hope your new phone makes you happy.'

And she was gone, walking away down the path, leaving Simon stood up on the cliff with eleven bulging shopping gathered around his feet.

***

The sun had dipped into the sea by the time Simon dropped off the last of the shopping bags to his slightly bemused customers. He'd had to hide the bags behind a rock up on the path and carry them down four at a time to various residents of the town. Two more of the bags had split open on the journey.

He'd refused to pocket the money from Maisie. He kept it clenched in his sweaty hand as he carried plastic bags this way and that throughout the town. He was annoyed at her for giving him the money. He was more annoyed at himself for running after it like an addict hearing the flush of a toilet.

It just didn't make sense. He'd stayed up all night figuring out exactly what she had to do to get her dream job. Then he'd found a way of actually paying for it and all she could say was no. She was supposed to be the criminal out of the two of them. He was the squeaky clean goodie-two-shoes and she was the wild child. So why was it that *he* was the one suggesting this stuff? And what made her think she had the moral high ground to say no?

But by the time Simon was carrying the last set of bags down the path into town his frustration gave way to tiredness. He'd spent the previous evening shouting, then hadn't slept all night and spent all day carrying other people's groceries. Maybe his exhausted brain *was* being ridiculous. A heist? The word was starting to seem as crazy as it sounded.

He was just Simon. Some kid from London living with his aunt and uncle. He wasn't George Clooney, he wasn't Brad Pitt. He couldn't even pick crabs out of a rock pool without getting his fingers pinched. And besides there was no way he could do it without Maisie and she'd made her views pretty clear.

His heart sank a little. He'd only been trying to help. She'd seemed pretty bashful when she told him about her jumper dream. All he'd wanted to do was make her happy and he'd gone and messed that up too.

A bag ripped. A tin of beans rolled forlornly down the street and stopped at the door to the pub. Simon followed it, feeling all of the weight of his day settling on his shoulders at once. He stooped to pick it up just as the pub door opened and a man stumbled straight into him.

'Ya fuckin' watch it, yeah?'

The voice sounded familiar. It was that same voice he'd heard singing in the streets on many a late night. The man was bigger in person. His mop of curly hair was again tied up out of his eyes. A couple of strands were loose. He had a cigarette between his teeth. There was something familiar in his features.

'I'm sorry.'

'Yeah, ya better be. Little shit.'

He was slurring pretty badly even though it couldn't much late than six in the evening. He kicked the can of beans off down the street and pulled out a lighter. Simon tried to siddle past him to go and get the can. The man threw his lighter at a bin and missed.

'Fuckin' typical… ya got a light?'

'I'm sorry?'

'Have. You. Got. A. Fucking. Lighter?'

'No, sorry.'

'Sorry!'

The man put on a high quavering voice. Simon hoped he hadn't sounded like that.

'Fuckin' useless.'

Simon grabbed the can off the ground and walked quickly away into the night. He didn't hear footsteps following him. He walked the long way around to the final delivery house so he wouldn't pass the pub again. From a few streets away he heard the man singing into the impending night.

'I bet my heaaaaart on a fruity… and it done threw it all away… but I'll get money when I go 'ome… my little darlin' giiiirl will pay!'

***

Aunt Bella didn't ask how his day had been. Simon was glad because he wasn't quite sure he had the energy to hold a conversation. The three of them ate in silence. Simon struggled to keep his eyes open at the dimly lit table. He made an effort to finish everything on his plate though. If he was going to get back into his aunt's good books he'd have to start somewhere.

Just as he was getting up from the table Uncle Aled grabbed his arm. It was a soft grip but Simon could feel the power behind it. He sat back down. Uncle Aled stood, looked pointedly from Aunt Bella to Simon and back again, cleared the plates off the table and went to wash up in the other room. It was Aunt Bella who spoke first.

'He's right.'

'I'm so sorry.'

'I am too, sweetie.'

'No, I'm the one who should be apologising. I've not been acting like myself. I'm… I shouldn't have lied to you.'

Aunt Bella found his hand and squeezed it.

'Aled and I were talking last night. He... he says that kids - sorry, young people - need time to find out who they are. It's been so long that I forgot.'

'I shouldn't have lied about the job though. Or about seeing Maisie.'

'You... you can spend time with her. If you want to make jumpers, make jumpers.'

Simon gave her a dry smile. There was something sad and small in the smile Aunt Bella returned.

'Sweetie, you're an adult now. You make your own decisions. I'll stop getting in the way.'

'What did you mean when you said there are things I don't know about Maisie?'

Aunt Bella sighed and looked at their hands, still clasped together.

'In Wales we've got a saying. Your mum probably says it all the time. The old know and the young suspect. But who's to say which of them is right?'

She came back to reality and tapped him lightly on the back of the hand.

'It's in the past now. You should probably go straight to bed, sweetie. I won't be around tomorrow so you boys will have to fend for yourselves. God help you.'

Simon laughed. After a few more seconds they separated their hands and he got up from the table. He paused in the doorway then came back in to give his aunt a little hug. She hummed softly.

Chapter 9

Simon arrived at the beach early. He watched the sky turn pastel pink. The clouds smouldered and a golden spot appeared on the horizon. It stretched into a short line before lazily floating up out of the waters and into the sky.

Maisie was late. He didn't have a phone to check the time but she should've definitely arrived by now. The money from the previous evening was still scrunched up in his hand. The sun had cleared the water and was finding its way up into the clouds and still no sign of her.

He had a bucket with him. Maybe she was just running late and he should get started on the crabs by himself. Something didn't feel right though. Wasn't it always Maisie telling him not to be late? And yet as a couple of morning dog walkers appeared on the cliff, waving to him, there was no tangle of curly hair or homemade jumper with them.

In fact, as Simon waited, another man appeared on the beach. One who drove down the cliff in a Land Rover. He tipped his cap to Simon as he opened the boot and lifting out a large tub. The man walked down to the water's edge. The tide had been in when Simon arrived, kissing his toes. Now the water's edge was somewhere far in front of him. Five crab cages lay exposed by the rocks.

The man walked over to the cages and tipped each of them, one by one, into his tub. He looked markedly impressed with his haul as he walked back towards Simon and the car.

'Good catch this morning, lad.'

'Yeah?'

'Crab's a been a bit small recently but look a' these beauties. Primers, the lot of 'em.'

Simon peered into the tub with what he hoped was a look of surprise. No crabs for him today then.

'You got a name, lad? Don't think I've seen you round here before.'

'Simon.'

'Roger. Folks call me Jonesy.'

Satisfied and whistling to himself, Jonesy hopped up into his Land Rover and drove off back over the hill leaving Simon alone once again.

He watched a boat crawl along the horizon.

A figure appeared up on the path heading out of town. A little figure with tangled hair and a knitted jumper. She ducked away as quickly as she appeared but not before Simon spotted her.

'Maise!'

But she didn't reappear.

'Maisie, I know you're there.'

Still nothing.

'Look, I've got your money here. You proved your point, okay? You're right. No more… H-E-I-S-T.'

A little northern voice called back to him. It didn't have its usual punch.

'Good thing no one in this town knows how to spell.'

She still didn't appear though so Simon hiked up the path to where the voice had come from. He found her sat behind a rock. Something was wrong. This time she was the one with the bags under her eyes. What's more they looked swollen and red. She had one hand clutched to her side as she offered him a weak grin.

'Oh my god, Maisie.'

'I'm fine.'

She winced.

'Like hell you are. What's wrong? What happened?'

'It's nothing.'

'Maisie.'

'I'm okay, really.'

But as she stood up to face him, Simon could see her teeth clamping down on her bottom lip.

'Maisie, what happened? Was it... Did your dad do this?'

She didn't say anything. She didn't have to.

'Sit down.'

'Nah, it's fine. We'll get the crabs.'

'Mate, it's like 8:30. The crabs are gone.'

'Did you just say 'mate'? The north's rubbing off on you.'

'Sit down right now or I'll show you just how northern I can be.'

She laughed a little and finally lowered herself back onto the grass.

'Show me where it hurts.'

'What are you, a doctor?'

'Not if I have to deal with patients like you. Come on, I'm trying to help.'

'Fine.'

Simon could see the problem as soon as Maisie lifted the hem of her jumper and shirt. The was a dark hazy bruise on her lower left rib cage. He immediately felt out of his depth.

'Like what you see, doc?'

Maisie tried to laugh but only ended up wincing. She took a hesitant peek at the bruise herself and her face sobered slightly.

'Ah you know, that *is* lookin' worse.'

'What did he do?'

'It was his knee, I think.'

'Why?'

Maisie sighed. Her expression told him she didn't want to answer but he waited anyway.

'He, uh… he was at the pub last night. Fruit machine wasn't spinning right so popped home for some money from me but…'

Simon's stomach dropped. He finished the sentence for her.

'But you gave me what you made yesterday.'

'Mhm.'

'Maisie…'

'Don't. Let's just leave it, yeah?'

'You've got to tell someone.'

'I just did and look at all the help you're being.'

She tried to smile but stopped when Simon didn't smile back.

'So what's the prognosis, doc?'

'The prognosis is you're coming with me.'

'You ain't taking me to hospital.'

'How did I know you'd say that?'

'I ain't goin'.'

'Well, I'm not taking you. I've got someone better anyway. Come here.'

Simon hooked an arm around her back and lifted her to her feet as gently as he could. They fell into step with one another as they followed the path back into town.

***

If Uncle Aled had been surprised when he opened the door he didn't show it. He looked at Simon. He looked at Maisie and he stepped aside for them to come in. They went through to the kitchen where Uncle Aled pulled out up chair for Maisie to sit in, right under the kitchen light. She walked to it herself, leaving Simon stood in the doorway.

Uncle Aled pulled grabbed a chair of his own and faced her.

'It's, uh, nice to meet you, sir. I'm Maisie.'

'Aled.'

'Simon's overreacting, it's really not all that bad.'

She winced on the last word. Uncle Aled raised his eyebrows.

'Alright, it's uh… it's here.'

Maisie lifted her jumper and t-shirt up above the bruise and glanced down at it. Simon caught a flicker of uncertainty in her steady eyes. Uncle Aled leaned in and looked at the the purple blotch.

'Hm. Simon, ice.'

Simon jumped at his name and hesitated in the doorway momentarily. Ice? Where was he supposed to find ice? He took a couple of step towards the freezer but Uncle Aled stopped him.

'No. Garage.'

The fishing gear. Right. That made more sense, there was a freezer full of it back there. Simon was almost out of the room when his uncle stopped him again.

'Bag?'

'Oh. Right, yeah.'

Simon grabbed a plastic bag from the side and went out to the garage.

When he returned, Uncle Aled was laughing. It was that same hearty laugh that warmed the whole house whenever it rang out. Maisie had a grin on her face too and had to hide a giggle when she saw Simon in the doorway with a bag of ice cubes.

'What's so funny?'

Neither of them said anything. Instead they just laughed harder. Simon could feel himself going red.

'It's not about me, is it?'

Maisie was grimacing with pain but couldn't stop herself from giggling. Their wooden chairs were squeaking.

'Oh no, don't worry about me. I'll just take the ice back to the garage since you clearly don't need it anymore.'

Uncle Aled wiped a tear from under his eye and snatched the bag from Simon's indignant grasp. Very gently he placed it against Maisie's bruise and she tensed up slightly from the chill before settling back into her chair with a smirk.

'You going to tell me what's so funny?'

'Oh, you guessed it already.'

'You were laughing at me? What did I do?'

'Ah don't worry.'

Uncle Aled was chuckling slightly as got up from the table.

'So what's wrong with her?'

'Cracked ribs.'

'Does that mean we should take her to the hospital?'

His uncle just shook his head and disappeared off into another room, leaving Simon and Maisie alone in the kitchen together. Maisie was looking round at all of the chintzy decor in the room. There were a couple of pictures of cats hanging up on the wall. She leaned back in her chair, ice pack at her side and chewed her lip. After a moment, she stopped and looked Simon dead in the eyes.

'You know what? Fuck it. Let's do it.'

'Let's do what?'

'The heist.'

'Keep it down, Maisie. What if Uncle Aled heard?'

'Let's do the heist!'

'Sshh!'

'I'm serious, let's do it. Let's go rob a supermarket.'

'Why've you suddenly changed your mind?'

Simon could see tears pricking her eyes when she answered.

'Because I'm sick of this, alright? Look, you've only been here a couple of weeks. I've been stuck here for *years*. I'm sick of living with dad. I'm sick of stealing from people. I'm sick of being broke. I'm sick of being bored everyday. Somehow *you're* the most exciting person in this town. That shows how shit it is. So if you want to rob a supermarket, let's rob a supermarket.'

'Can we talk about this somewhere else? Somewhere where my uncle isn't within a ten foot radius?'

Maisie sprang to her feet and made a beeline for the front door. She called out over her shoulder to him.

'Bring that notepad, we've got some planning to do.'

***

The pair of them walked and talked. The followed the footpath out of town towards the next town over, the home of the fabled supermarket, and then looped back, cutting inland up the hills and then down, back to where they came from.

'Maisie, we can't actually do it though. You were right yesterday. It was a dumb idea that I came up with while running on no sleep.'

'Yeah and now *I'm* running on no sleep and I'm saying yes.'

'And I'm saying no. Look, you said it yourself, what if we get caught? You're not exactly in a fit state to be stealing stuff right now.'

'I dunno, we won't get caught. Mate, you're supposed to be the smart one here. You came up with the plan in first place, you'll figure something out.'

'What, I'm the smart one who came up with the plan that'll almost definitely get us arrested?'

'*Almost* definitely.'

'Maisie, are you sure about this?'

'Hundred percent... eighty, maybe sixty, but that's pretty high for me.'

Simon chewed his lip. Maisie punched him in the arm so hard he almost dropped his pen.

'Ow.'

'Mate, come on! It'll be fun. What happened to all that talk about followin' your dreams? Look, if your maths is right then this could start an actual business for me. I could stop getting up at 5am to steal crabs and start getting up at 5am to knit jumpers.'

'Has anyone ever told you how weird you are?'

'Has anyone ever told you how boring you are? Look, you could buy like a car or something. Or start paying rent on your own place. You could fly to Japan. If you need to prove to your mum that you're a proper adult, it doesn't come much better than that. I'm not letting you get cold feet on me, alright?'

'I'm... I just... if, *if* we were going to do it, hypothetically, we'd have to figure out a way of stealing everything without anyone suspecting it was us.'

'Well, yeah.'

'We'd need damn good alibis because we'd be... *you'd* be the prime suspect.'

'Sure.'

'That means ideally we wouldn't even be there when the place gets robbed.'

'Right.'

'I doubt the police round here get much action so they'd probably pour all they have into finding the culprit so we need to be airtight.'

'Yeah.'

'In fact, it's probably best we just don't get them involved in the first place. But that, that's a big ask. Like, a *big* ask. We'd need a whole team of people working on this. Not just us.'

'Who?'

Simon shrugged.

'This is all hypothetical of course.'

Maisie just smiled at him and took a seat on a rock by the footpath. She looked pretty tired. Simon returned her smile and sat down next to her. They watched the sea as it folded neat little waves in front of them. The jumper flapped around on the fence behind them.

'Maisie, are you sure that you-'

'Yes.'

'Okay then.'

They watched the sea for a few minutes, both too absorbed in thought to put anything into words. This really was a dumb idea but it wasn't impossible. And if Maisie wanted to do it then that was that.

Simon opened his notebook to the first page. Scrawled across it were all the meticulous notes Aaron had made him write. Notes about the supermarket, the tills, how the business operated, shift times, all of it. For the first time his old boss had come in handy. Maisie piped up next to him.

'Can we wear disguises?'

'Disguises?'

'Yeah. In all the movies they always dress up in cool outfits.'

'What like suits and ball gowns?'

'Mate, could you imagine me ever wearing a ball gown? Nah, I was thinking boiler suits or SWAT gear.'

'I mean, we might stick out dressed as a two man SWAT team out here.'

'Yeah, you're probably right.'

Simon looked back down at his notebook and finished reading the page he'd been on. When he turned to the next, a sheet of paper fell out. It was the leaflet that he'd been given on his second day at the supermarket from the school right across the road.

Fancy Dress Village Fete!
All ages welcome.
Egg Hunt, Face Paint, Bake Sale, and much more!
Bowen Primary School.

'Maisie.'

'Yeah, what's up?'

'Maybe disguises are on the cards after all.'

***

The pair of them sat on that rock for hours, spitballing ideas. Everything from hiring an industrial bulldozer to 'accidentally' crash into the supermarket to recruiting an army of school children to all rush the shop at once. Before long Simon found himself laughing, properly laughing. He couldn't remember the last time he'd sat down with a friend and just talked and joked until his ribs ached. Maisie's ribs were clearly aching much more than his though but that didn't stop her cracking jokes the whole time.

The sun set. The cold set in. Maisie's ice had melted. Simon flipped the notebook shut and stood.

'Uncle Aled's probably starting to wonder where I've got to.'

'We don't have to go home yet though?'

'It's getting late and I'm starving.'

'Can't we stay here a bit longer?'

There was something in Maisie's voice. Something behind her words. Something small and sad. Home for her didn't mean the same thing as home for him. Simon sat back down on the rock. Their shoulders were touching slightly. He could hear Maisie's delicate breathing. She was pretty good at hiding how much pain she was in.

'Will your dad be pissed when you get home?'

'Pissed as in drunk or as in pissed off?'

'Both. Either.'

'Both, probably.'

'Do you ever think of running away? Moving out?'

'I can't.'

Neither of them said anything for a while. The breeze died down.

'Look, he needs me. If I wasn't around there'd be no one to pay rent. No one to calm him down when he goes off on one. No one to put him in the recovery position when he passes out. He'd choke on his own vomit within a week and no one would even look for him.'

'That's not fair on you.'

'It's not.'

'Isn't there somewhere he can go?'

Simon didn't want to say it but Maisie did for him.

'You mean prison? Yeah. He's done enough to earn a spot there, that's for sure.'

'Do you ever think...?'

'Could you do that? To your own family I mean, could you do that?'

Simon didn't answer. Maisie tipped her head back and looked up at the stars.

'One day... one day when I'm rich and famous, I'll get a fat old house. Or maybe like a New York apartment. Like a proper place to live. And I'll sit outside in the evening and stare up at the stars with some proper champagne in my hand. And I'll have like five dogs. Then I'll've made it.'

'I'm more of a cat person.'

'Course you are.'

Simon grinned. As the evening stretched by, more stars came out to join them.

'You never see the sky like this back in London. Too much light all the time.'

'Makes you feel small doesn't it?'

'But good small.'

'Good small. Yeah.'

'Which one's Libra?'

'Mate, I can point out the moon and that's about it. Doesn't this mean I'm supposed to hate you?'

'Why?'

'I'm Aries. Isn't that how it goes? We're supposed to hate each other.'

'Huh, I guess that's the first time horoscopes have ever got something right.'

Maisie elbowed him. Simon almost did it back then remember her ribs. Probably best not to. Wait, Aries?

'Hang on, doesn't that mean it's your birthday around now.'

'Mhm.'

'Oh shit, it's not today is it?'

'Nah, don't worry. It was on the 17th.'

'Of April?'

'Yeah.'

'So that was…'

'Don't worry about it.'

'Maisie, that was last Friday! I was with you, that was my first day on the job. When we were clearing out Penny's house.'

'Uh-huh.'

'Why didn't you say something?'

'I mean, I did try but you talked over me.'

'When?'

'When you asked how old I was. I was like 'I'm eighteen, my birthday is…' and you were like 'I'm nineteen, ha ha ha!''

'Oh my god, I'm so sorry.'

'It's not a big deal… Genuinely, it's not. Stop looking so guilty!'

'I'm so sorry.'

'It's fine. Birthdays are never really a big thing for me anyways.'

'Did you get any presents? A cake?'

'It's not a big deal.'

'Maisie.'

'Just forget about it alright? There's always next year.'

Simon frowned.

'Stop looking so sour! It's fine, honestly. Look, you're right it's probably time we go home now.'

'We haven't made any money today. What if your dad asks for some?'

'I'll figure something out.'

'That's not fair.'

'I've got by for eighteen years. I can last a bit longer.'

'Oh, I almost forgot.'

Simon handed her the scrunched up wad of cash back. She took it as he helped her up off the rock. She looked dead on her feet.

'You can always come and stay with me and Uncle Aled tonight?'

'Thanks but I can't.'

'Maisie.'

'Dad needs me. I can't leave him alone.'

'Okay, if you're sure.'

'Think I am.'

They started walking down the path side by side. Simon's notebook was sticking out of his back pocket. Maisie took another look up at the stars as they walked.

'If this heist of yours works, I'll move out. I'll get a flat and I'll sell my jumpers.'

'Promise?'

'Promise.'

They disappeared down the path leading into town.

***

Simon needed sleep. He knew that but as he lay in bed his eyes wouldn't stay closed for more than a few seconds at a time. Uncle Aled had made them fish for dinner. No vegetables, no potatoes, just fish. Fried up and salted.

Honestly, he wasn't quite sure how he felt. Both about his dinner and about his day. Neither of them sat quite right with him. He looked at the clock. It had just turned Thursday. He'd have to be back down at the beach in about six hours, assuming Maisie would be there. The sooner they could get this money, the better.

His imagination drifted through all the possibilities of what he could buy with his share of the cash. Before long his imagination grew up into dreams that put a smile on his face until morning. Somewhere further along the coast Maisie lay awake, her ribs jabbing her every time she found herself drifting off.

Chapter 10

'Why did you tell me about the job in the supermarket?'

'You what?'

'The other week, you were the one who told me they were hiring there. How come?'

Maisie grinned.

'You really wanna know?'

'Yeah.'

'Alright, I knew the manager was a knob because he tried to hire me already. Super creepy guy. Plus I thought you'd be a massive pushover who'd let me get away with stealing... Oh come on, don't cry about it.'

'You really thought I was a pushover?'

'I still do, mate.'

'Funny. We'll see how much of a pushover I am in a minute, won't we.'

They were standing across the road from the supermarket leaning against the school gates. They had about a week before they'd be enacting the greatest robbery the Welsh coast had ever seen. Or at least that's what it was in

Simon's head. Maisie was looking at the automatic doors, concern scrunching up her face.

'You sure this is a good idea?'

'It'll be fine.'

'Won't it be a bit suspicious?'

'Aaron's an idiot. If I walked in with a pair of glasses and moustache right now he'd probably introduce himself.'

'Okay.'

'I'll go in, demand that he pays me for the work I did and try to get a look at that safe. We need to know where it is and how big it is.'

He was talking more for his own benefit at this point than Maisie's. He shut himself up, balled up his fists then unclenched them quickly. He needed Maisie to think he knew what he was doing, as if he planned heists every other week and this was no big deal. Just get in, look at the safe, get out. With any luck Aaron would already be in his office so Simon could just walk right in and leave.

He flashed Maisie a quick smile and strode off across the street. The automatic doors gave their familiar squeak as they welcomed him in. Aaron blocked his path immediately.

'Well, well, well. If it isn't Simpson.'

Simon couldn't have imagined Aaron saying anything less cliched if he tried.

'What's got you crawling back here tail between your legs, huh?'

'I was wondering if we could talk in private.'

'Oh like how you quit in private? Oh wait, you didn't. Did you?'

'I didn't come here for an argument.'

'Oh yeah? Then what did you come here for, Simpson?'

'Well, I came because you're a smart and reasonable business man and I wanted to talk to you.'

The words felt sour on his lips but they made Aaron leer at him.

'Aight. You ever been to my office, Simpson?'

'No, sir.'

'Well then boy, you're in for a treat today.'

Simon followed him through the aisles. They passed Phil, who was leaning against the wall by the back door. Simon nodded to him. Phil stared right on through him.

The office in the back was an ugly box of a room. There was a roaring tower computer sat on the desk, a outdated naked calendar on the wall and three dead plants. The air smelled of sweat. It was somehow humid in here even though the door and window were both open. Aaron strutted round the desk and sank into a chair that was far too big for him.

'You got balls, boy. I'll give you that. Walking back in here after that little stunt you pulled.'

'I'm sorry for walking out so abruptly. It wasn't professional.'

'So is that it? You've come to get your job back?'

There was a hint of glee in Aaron's voice.

'Because believe you me that ain't never happening as long as-'

'I don't want the job back.'

'Oh, well… good. Because you can't have it.'

'Okay.'

'Well? What do you want then?'

Simon couldn't see the safe anywhere in the room. Aaron had said it was in the back office right? Maybe he'd moved it. Or maybe it was under the desk.

'I want my money.'

Aaron tipped back his head and laughed. It was utterly unconvincing. An attempt at a supervillain's laugh that just sounded a bit forced and awkward.

No safe in the corners or by the door. Where was it?

'Simpson, oh Simpson! You're having me on.'

'I worked here for two and half days, I'm owed £132.50.'

'You're owed *this.*'

Aaron stuck two fingers in the air, giggling at his joke. The safe must be under the desk. Surely.

'I don't see what's so funny.'

'Boy, you haven't got a foot to stand on. I ain't paying you shit.'

'Really?'

'Really.'

'I was hoping that we could be civil about this.'

'Civil? Boy, what do you know about civil?'

'Well, I might not know much about being civil but I do know a bit about your finances here.'

Aaron's smile vanished.

'That got your attention.'

'You don't scare me, boy.'

'I really don't care if I scare you or not. All I care about is walking out of that door with £132.50 in my back pocket.'

'And where do you suppose that money'll be coming from.'

'The safe under your desk.'

He'd taken a gamble. The words had come out before he'd had time to reconsider. Judging by the look on Aaron's face though, he'd guessed right.

'What safe?'

'The one where you hoard the money you steal from the tills every night. The one the local police might take a keen interest in.'

'Is that a threat?'

'Yes. Yes, actually that was a direct threat. Pay me now, or I go straight to the station.'

Aaron's moustache wriggled this way and that. He licked it. The saliva slicked the hairs to his skin.

'You've got balls.'

'And you don't. Now I'd like to take my money and leave please.'

Aaron stared at him for a long moment. Simon met his gaze. No one moved.

Then Aaron reached down to his right. Simon tried to quickly sidle round the desk to get a peek at the safe. It was small, small enough to carry, with a keypad on the front. Aaron paused with his finger on the first button. 9.

'A bit of privacy, yeah?'

Simon had been too eager. Seeing the code would've been a great bonus but there was no way he'd find it now. Aaron was eying him up and down, running his tongue along his front teeth. Simon raised his hands apologetically and tried to look casually up at the ceiling.

Beep. Beep. Beep. Beep. Beep. Beep.

Six numbers. The first one probably a 9. That was a start at least. Still, cracking the safe open was a problem for later. As long as they could carry it out of there, that would be good enough. He heard the door open and the creak of Aaron's chair as he reached inside. Simon looked back at the weaselly little man with a small stack of notes in his hand.

'£130.'

'Seriously?'

'You take it and get out.'

'£150.'

'No way. We agreed on £130.'

'I demanded £132.50. Now I want £150. Actually make it £200.'

'£200? That's extortion.'

'It's blackmail actually but right now, Aaron, you don't have a foot to stand on.'

The moustache wilted.

***

'Still think I'm a pushover?'

'You're lying.'

'Count it yourself, £200 right here.'

'Is it actually? You know what? Fair enough. Was he pissed?'

'I've never seen anyone that red faced in my life.'

Simon had a skip in his step as they walked along the coastal path. Maisie was looking much healthier than she'd been the previous day. They didn't really have a plan for today, other than coming up with an idea for their heist. That was why they were so surprised when Aunt Bella appeared around the corner.

'Simon, sweetie! I didn't catch you this morning.'

'Aunt Bella, hi.'

'So what are you two up to? Working hard?'

There was something accusatory in her voice.

'We, um… we're having a meeting.'

'Ah! Well, don't let me get in the way.'

She squeezed Simon's shoulder as she walked past. Neither she nor Maisie acknowledged each other.

'Oh actually sweetie, before you go, I was wondering if you'd like to invite Maisie along for tea tonight?'

Simon stuttered for a few seconds, convinced he'd misheard his aunt. Maisie stepped in for him.

'That's really kind but I'm fine.'

'Nonsense. Simon, she's welcome isn't she?'

'Um, yeah? Yeah, of course she is - I mean, you are.'

'Perfect! We'll eat at 7:30. Lamb casserole. Have fun with your meeting!'

And with that, Aunt Bella was off down the path behind them. Simon shook his head to check if that had really just happened.

'She didn't ask if I was vegetarian.'

'You aren't, are you?'

'No dickhead but it's the principle, isn't it?'

'What the hell just happened? That was an ambush if ever I've seen one.
'Yup.'

'Look, you don't have to come.'

'Looks like I do.'

'I could make up an excuse.'

'No, it's fine. I'll come.'

'You sure?'

'Sure. I can see how the other half live.'

'Hey, I'm as broke as you right now.'

'Mate, you just made two hundred quid because you asked for it.'

'Not so loud, Aunt Bella might still hear us.'

'Lamb casserole, huh? I can deal with that. Is she a good cook?'

'I mean, yeah.'

'Well, if it all goes to shit at least I get a good square meal before she kills me with a dessert spoon.'

'Why does she hate you so much?'

Maisie sighed. The smile faded. She looked old. Older than Simon. Almost as old as the cliff they were walking on.

'You actually wanna know? It might... I dunno, it might change some things. Like how you see me and that. I s'pose it's probably better if I tell you though instead of having her do it. Only if you want to hear this though.'

'You didn't steal her favourite scarf did you?'

Maisie didn't laugh at his joke. She was staring at the sea, as if she was waiting for it to send an enormous wave up to wash her away from the conversation. But the wave didn't come.

'Your aunt hates me because she thinks I did something.'

'Okay?'

She didn't elaborate for a long time. When she did it was all in a rush, like how she always was when she was nervous. Kind of like ripping off a plaster.

'Me and dad moved here five years ago. It was just before Huw died. Dad met him a couple of times in the pub. They drank together. Like, a lot. One night, Huw lost his wallet and went looking for it out on the cliff when he'd had too many and... well, yeah. You know the rest.'

'I... what've you got to do with it?'

'Your aunt blames me and dad for it.'

'That's... that's ridiculous. He died because the cliff fell in. He was in the wrong place at the wrong time, alright? That wasn't his fault. It wasn't your dad's fault and it definitely isn't yours.'

Maisie wasn't looking at him. Simon grabbed her arm and went round to face her.

'Maisie, that's not your fault. Okay? Whatever problems Aunt Bella's got they're not because of you. They're her problems to deal with. You got that?'

'Mhm.'

'Maisie.'

'Yeah, sure.'

But he could tell he hadn't gotten through to her. She just kept staring off past him into the sea. From here they could just about make out the tiny white walled graveyard with its mismatching headstones, stood too close to the cliff's edge.

***

They spent the rest of the day planning the heist in the pub. It was quiet during the day, quiet enough that anyone could overhear them, but Maisie led him through a door, round a winding corridor, through another door, down some stairs, and out into a hidden downstairs area. It was a small, long room, built into the ground with a huge map of the Welsh coast on one wall and various nautical decorations leading to a set of open doors at the opposite end. Out of those doors was a tiny balcony below street level just above the river as it rushed out to meet the sea.

Simon was about to ask Maisie how on Earth she'd known that this room existed when the logical part of his brain kicked in and put two and two together. They settled down on the table right by the giant map. On it they could see every street, country lane, and path that spread out from the towns like veins from the heart. Right there in the middle of the small town was the pub, in the centre of the big town was the supermarket with the school field right across the road.

Simon opened his notepad and put the flier for the fete where they could both read it. Then frantically started to write down everything he could remember about the safe in Aaron's office, the make, the dimensions, the location. Once he was convinced he'd written out just about everything he could think of, he lowered the pen and looked across at Maisie. She was staring at the flier intently. He could see the cogs turning.

'What are you thinking, Maisie?'

'You said yesterday that I'll be the number one suspect right?'

'Yeah.'

'But I reckon after your little meeting with Aaron today, you'll be up there in his suspicions too.'

'Yeah.'

'So, we'll need to be somewhere the whole time, right? Somewhere visible where the whole town can see what we're up to.'

'So what are you thinking?'

'I'm thinking, how in the hell are we supposed to steal £10,000 in cash when the entire town is watching us?'

'Well... what if we don't?'

'Mate, we've been over this. You're not getting cold feet again.'

'No, no. Listen, I'm not saying we don't steal the money. I'm saying *we* don't steal the money.'

'Well, who else is taking it for us? I don't know about you but I don't fancy going door to door asking pensioners to help us commit a crime.'

Simon sighed. With £200 in his pocket, suddenly the heist didn't seem so necessary. In fact, it was feeling more and more impossible by the minute. He looked at the map. Maisie was right. They weren't in London or Vegas. They were in the middle of nowhere, Wales. They were surrounded by sea or fields in every direction. There were no men in black suits carrying guns everywhere. They were amongst farmers, old people and school kids. Quite possible the last group of people you'd expect to be involved in a heist.

'Hang on.'

'What?'

'I think I might have something.'

'Mate, what is it?'

'Do you remember the London riots?'

'Uh-huh.'

'I remember seeing something on the news about it where the police couldn't arrest everyone. There were too many people involved that they were just completely outnumbered. Didn't have enough cells, guards, or anything.'

'Sure.'

'They couldn't arrest a whole city.'

'What? And they can't arrest a whole town either?'

'Not around here they can't.'

'So what, we start a riot in the nursing home?'

'Not exactly.'

'I hate it when you do this.'

'Do what?'

'You know what. Just spit it out.'

'Alright, imagine this. We somehow get someone else to go in and take the money. Then that person unknowingly gives it out to just about every person at the fete. Then we make it so that over the course of the day all of that cash slowly filters through to you and me.'

'Sure. Except how are we possibly going to make someone unknowingly steal £10,000 from a safe and then convince the whole town to give all of that money to us?'

'I haven't thought about that bit yet.'

'Right.'

'But it's a start.'

'Oh yeah sure.'

'We'll figure it out.'

Maisie wasn't looking at him anymore. She was playing with her sleeve again.

'Listen, Maisie, about tonight. You don't have to come if you don't want to.'

'I'll be there.'

'Are you sure?'

'I'll be there.'

***

Sure enough, at 7:30 precisely that evening, Maisie was there. Simon had sat in the front room for the last half hour waiting. He thought it was probably for the best if he got to the door first. He'd been expecting the bell but instead heard a muffled tapping sound from the hallway. He shot out of the room and had to stop himself with his hand on the door handle. He waited a couple of seconds before opening it.

The girl in front of him did not look like Maisie. He'd got so used to seeing her in those crazy knitted jumpers that seeing her in normal clothes looked anything but. She had a pair of dark jeans on and a silky yellow shirt. Her hair had clearly got into a fight with a brush and she had a small silver necklace on her chest.

When Simon met her eyes he was most shocked of all. She was wearing makeup. He didn't think he'd ever seen her wearing even a hint of it before. He felt slightly ashamed at how surprised he was. He would have expected Maisie's makeup to look a little bit like a five year old raiding her mother's handbag but it was actually kind of nice. It was subtle and neat and made her look like an actual girl.

'Oh God, you hate it.'

'No, no!'

'You do. I look stupid don't I? It's the top isn't it? I'll go home and change.'

'No, Maisie, you look... um, fine.'

He kicked himself. Why couldn't he just say it?

'I don't though.'

'No, no, you do. I swear.'

'Oh God, this was dumb. I shouldn't've come here. Look, I'll go home. Tell them I was sick and...'

But it was too late. A hand appeared on Simon's shoulder and threw him out of the way. Aunt Bella took his place on the porch surveying Maisie who stood half a foot lower, in the little pool of light spilling out of the house.

'Oh sweetie, you look lovely!'

Maisie stood still for a second, unsure what to do with the compliment. Simon half expected her to bolt down the street at any moment. His conscience twinged. How come Aunt Bella could say that and he got all tongue tied? Maisie tried to tug at her sleeve but the usual loose thread hanging there from her jumper was gone.

'D'you think? It's not too much?'

'Of course it's not! You look like a movie star.'

Aunt Bella floated down the stairs and whisked Maisie under her arm and into the house, leaving Simon stood alone amongst the discarded shoes. The night air whispered something to him but he was already closing the door and didn't hear it in time.

The smell of lamb casserole led Simon into the dining room. Maisie and Aunt Bella were already sat at the table when he arrived. He did a small doubletake; Aunt Bella was clasping Maisie's hand in hers.

'...and of course, sweetie, you're always welcome to come round for dinner. Goodness knows Simon leaves enough food on his plate for someone else.'

'That's really kind of you.'

'And if you ever need a lift anywhere Aled's got the car. You know, if you ever fancy a day trip to Cardiff, you two, it's not a problem.'

'Oh thank you.'

Simon noticed Maisie shifting in her chair slightly. Aunt Bella's grip on her hands looked slightly too tight.

'Oh, Simon sweetie, I didn't see you there. Sit down, sit down. You have a nasty habit of standing in my blind spots. I was just saying to Maisie that if you two ever need lift anywhere, Cardiff, Swansea, wherever, then you can just ask.'

'Oh, that's-'

'And where's Aled with the veg? Aled! Simon, sweetie, sorry for being a pain but could you run and see what's taking your uncle so long?'

'Sure, if you guys are fine in here?'

The question was aimed at Maisie but Aunt Bella cut across.

'And why wouldn't we be?'

'I... No, nothing. Don't worry.'

He tried to catch Maisie's eye as he got up from the table but Aunt Bella had already turned her stream of conversation back in that direction and Maisie looked like she was having a hard time just keeping up.

In the kitchen, Uncle Aled was draining the carrots. Simon stopped in the doorway.

'Would you like some help carrying stuff through?'

Uncle Aled grunted and shook his head. Simon watched as his uncle poured the steaming vegetables into a dish and carried it stoically through to the dining room. He was moving stiffly. His brow was furrowed slightly. Simon followed him back towards the sound of his aunt's voice.

'You know, sweetie, I actually had a friend who grew up around there. Clara. You remember Clara, don't you Aled?'

Uncle Aled grunted.

'Yes well she was something else, that girl. Always a bit of a wild one but I suppose that is the type you get up there isn't it?'

Maisie didn't answer. Aunt Bella ploughed on anyway.

'Must be something in the water, mustn't it? Aled, those carrots look delicious. Thank you so much. Right, well now that we're all here - sit down, Simon, come on - now that we're all here I think it's time to say grace… Maisie, would you do the honours?'

'Oh, I couldn't-'

'Nonsense! Of course you can.'

'Aunt Bella, I don't think it's fair-'

'Hush, Simon. Maisie, please.'

'She's our guest.'

'I know that sweetie but she's a big girl, she can speak for herself. Maisie, dear…'

'Aunt Bella.'

'Simon.'

But Uncle Aled's voice cut through silencing all of them.

'Jesus, thank you for dinner. Amen.'

'Okay then. Um, amen. Thank you, Aled.'

'Amen.'

'Amen.'

'Well then, tuck in everyone. Maisie, sweetie, pass me your plate. Careful it's hot.'

'It's not too bad.'

'Ah that's good, we wouldn't want to burn you would we? What kind of hospitality would that be? Now, is a bit of everything okay? Casserole, mash, veg?'

'Yeah, a bit of everything's great. Thanks.'

'And to drink?'

'Um, I don't know. What is there?'

'Well, there's water, sparkling and normal, orange juice, apple juice… hm, what else is there Simon?'

'Dunno.'

'I'm happy just having water.'

'Are you sure? Sparkling or still?'

'Uh, still is good.'

'Still water. Simon the jug's by you, would you mind?'

'Sure.'

Simon spilled a bit of water on the table as he poured the glass. Aunt Bella's eye snapped over to the little puddle but she looked away with a smile plastered on her face before anyone other than Simon noticed. He handed Maisie the glass and she took a hesitant sip just as Aunt Bella placed the steaming plate of food in front of her. It was loaded even higher than Simon's meals had ever been.

'Oh wow, this looks delicious. Thank you.'

'Well, you'd better have bigger appetite than young Simon here.'

'I'll definitely try.'

'Nonsense, eat it all. I insist.'

'Um, okay.'

Dutifully, Maisie tucked into her casserole but the first forkful had only just entered her mouth when Aunt Bella started questioning her.

'So, your father, what's he up to at the moment?'

Maisie tried to swallow the food as fast as she could to answer and grimaced slightly. She probably burned her mouth.

'Mm… sorry. He um, he's working odds and ends, you know?'

'No, I don't dear.'

'Um, well he's like a handyman, I guess.'

'Like a handyman?'

'He *is* a handyman.'

'Getting much work at the moment?'

'Not really.'

'Huh, that's a shame.'

Maisie waited for a moment but Aunt Bella didn't continue. Hesitantly she took another forkful of mash and started chewing.

'Simon tells us that you knit jumpers.'

This time Maisie didn't swallow her food straight away. She chewed it deliberately before answering. Simon decided to step in.

'She does. She knits all her own, the ones she wears around.'

'Is that so? I don't suppose you made that top you're wearing too?'

Maisie shook her head.

'Well I think you look lovely in it. It's a great improvement.'

Simon clenched his teeth.

'*I* like Maisie's jumpers. I think they look great.'

'Oh yes, sweetie. Of course, I didn't mean to say that they don't. They're just different is all. You must admit though Simon, sat here she looks like a proper young lady.'

Simon could feel himself going red. He didn't look across at Maisie.

'She, um… yeah. She looks great. She…'

He clenched his fists and finished off his sentence.

'Always looks great. In her jumpers and like she is now.'

He stole a glance at Maisie. That familiar little smile was twisting her lips. She was wearing lipstick. He took a plate and started to serve food onto it. Next to Maisie's mountain, his own looked like a kid's meal.

'Simon, sweetie, please take more.'

'It's fine. I'm not all that hungry.'

'You'll vanish in front of our eyes if you're not careful.'

Aunt Bella gave him a stern look but let it slide. Simon took his place beside Maisie again. For a while they ate in silence. The only sound in the room was the tentative clinking of metal on china. Simon noticed Maisie leaning back in her chair a bit more. He started to actually tuck into his food properly. Uncle Aled's shoulders dropped slightly.

The only light in the room was the warm glow coming from the bulb hanging low over the table. Maybe this meal wasn't such a bad idea after all. Aunt Bella set down her cutlery and wiped her mouth.

'So sweetie, where did you learn to knit? Did your mother teach you?'

'No, no. I taught myself. Didn't really have a mum around to teach me so…'

'Oh, I'm so sorry to hear that. At least you have your dad though.'

'He's um… yeah, he's still around.'

'So your knitting?'

'Right, yeah. I started a few years ago, around the time we moved to Wales. I was really shit at first but you know what they say about practice.'

Aunt Bella stiffened. Uncle Aled glanced at her. Simon had probably just witnessed the first swear word uttered in this house in decades. Maisie kept on talking, oblivious.

'It was kind of trial and error at first until I found a book in a car boot sale that gave me some tips. I think it was from about twenty years before I was born but it was actually pretty good. I still keep it by my bed. In fact, there's this new jumper that I've started working on with this really complicated cross stitch pattern that's a bit of a bitch-'

Aunt Bella squeaked. It was somewhere between a cough and a small scream, like a spurt of steam escaping from a pipe. Maisie stopped dead and looked across the table at her. Aunt Bella had turned a bright red.

'Oh, I'm sorry. Did I say something wrong?'

Simon answered before Aunt Bella could.

'Yeah, no it's fine, don't worry. It's just we don't really swear all that much round here.'

'Did I… wait.'

Maisie mouthed the word 'bitch' questioningly to him. Simon nodded.

'Oh right, I'm so sorry. I didn't mean to. I didn't realise.'

'It's quite alright, sweetie. Just remember, Jesus is in the room too.'

Maisie nodded and paused over her meal. She was about to take another bite when put her fork back down.

'Wait. Surely Jesus is in every room. Even the ones we swear in?'

'Well dear, we try not to swear in any rooms.'

'Why not?'

'I'm sorry.'

'Maisie…'

'No, seriously. Why not?'

'Well, I would think it's quite clear why not.'

'Surely we should be honest with God. Speak openly to Him and all that. Why would we censor ourselves for Him? If anything God's the only one who should hear us swearing since He knows our heart and all.'

'Maisie…'

'I'm right though. Do you think God's gonna be offended if I'm praying and go "Man, I've a shit day"? I reckon He'd be up there nodding like "Yeah mate, you really have".'

Veins were popping on the backs of Aunt Bella's hands. Simon kicked Maisie's leg but she kicked him back harder, smiling across at Aunt Bella all the while. Everyone in the room waited for Aunt Bella's response. After a few deep shaky breaths she returned Maisie's smile.

'Well dear, let's agree to disagree. But while we're in this house I would appreciate it if you didn't swear anymore.'

'Of course. Wouldn't want to upset Jesus now, would we?'

It was the first time Simon had ever seen his aunt look so visibly flustered. He wasn't sure whether to run or laugh. Maisie was tucking back into her food looking a little proud of herself. He couldn't help but realise that her plate was almost clean already. None of Aunt Bella's intimidation tactics really seemed like they were working on her. Aunt Bella was just opening her mouth to speak again when Simon butted in.

'Well, it looks like we're all just about done eating. Maisie, do you want to help me wash up?'

'Sweetie, we've only just started. You really don't need…'

'No, no. It's fine. We'll do it. Right Maisie?'

He kicked her again.

'Right. Thanks for tea, it was delicious.'

'Anytime dear.'

But something in Aunt Bella's voice made it sound like that was the furthest thing from the truth.

***

'What the hell was that?'

'What?'

'Don't you start that. Are you trying to make Aunt Bella hate you?'

'She already hates me.'

'Gee I wonder why.'

'Hey!'

'Is it really too much to ask for you to behave yourself. For five minutes?'

'I'm trying, okay?'

'Are you?'

'Look I didn't come here, all dressed up like a twat, for you to start yelling at me.'

'No you came here to start a fight apparently.'

'I'm *me*, okay? I'm Maisie. I swear, I say dumb shit, I'm annoying, everyone in this town hates me but at least I know who I am.'

'What's that supposed to mean?'

'Oh come on.'

'What?'

'You're the biggest wuss I've ever met in my life. When you're in church you pretend to be a good little Christian. When you're with your precious Aunt Bella you pretend to be all squeaky clean. When you're with me you pretend that you're hard, you start swearing, stealing and planning to rob supermarkets.'

'Keep your voice down.'

'Or what? They'll hear that you're not a perfect little goodie two shoes.'

'Maisie.'

'Or are you? Are you really a goodie two shoes who just pretends to be different around me?'

'I'm…'

'You're what? Because honestly I can't figure it out myself. I might be a piece of shit but at least I know what I am.'

Maisie paused for breath. They stood facing each other by the sink, the abandoned dirty dishes piled high. With her sleeves rolled up Maisie looked about ready to knock him out. Simon took a long time choosing his words before he replied.

'You're wrong, you know?'

'Am I now?'

'Not everyone in town hates you. If you opened up to people once in a while maybe you'd have some more friends.'

'Thanks for that sage advice.'

'Not everyone has to be your enemy, you know?'

'Yeah, well maybe they should.'

Tears were pricking her eyes. Simon realised too late that there was probably more to this than he'd thought.

'Maybe everyone should hate me. Yeah, even you. Maybe your aunt's right about everything.'

'What are you saying?'

'You seriously think I've opened up to you about everything?'

'What do you mean everything?'

There was a soft knock at the door. Uncle Aled was stood there, eyes on the floor. He grumbled and went back into the dining room.

'Pudding.'

Simon sighed and hung up the tea towel. It was still bone dry. They hadn't even turned the tap on yet. The fight went out of Maisie. She turned away to wipe her eyes. Simon pretended he hadn't seen.

'Maisie... I.... I'm sorry for yelling.'

'Mm.'

'And I'm sorry about Aunt Bella.'

He didn't entirely know what he meant by that but he knew there was definitely something in there for him to apologise about.

'Let's just get through pudding then I'll walk you home.'

'I can walk myself home.'

'I know you can. But I want to.'

Maisie grumbled but didn't argue. Instead she just rolled her sleeves back down and followed him back into the front room.

***

Maisie didn't say anything as they ate the cake and ice cream. Nor did Simon. Aunt Bella tried to start a few conversations but let them die when she realised how futile it was. Simon picked at his food. Any semblance of an appetite that he once had was gone. Maisie spooned the last of the melted ice cream into her mouth and wiped her hands on a napkin.

'That was delicious, thank you.'

'That's quite alright dear.'

'And I um... I just wanted to say that I guess I'm sorry for... you know.'

Aunt Bella face softened and a small smile appeared on her lips.

'I'm sorry too, sweetie.'

'No, no. I was in the wrong. I knew that you didn't like swearing and I kept doing it anyway just to pi- just to annoy you. So yeah, I'm sorry.'

'Thank you, dear.'

'It's getting late, I think I'll just head home if that's alright.'

'Absolutely dear. Thank you for coming.'

'Thanks for the meal. It was good. Really. Um, Simon?'

Simon smiled across at her. She gave him a little smile back and stood up. Something fell out of her pocket and thudded heavily on the floor. Maisie darted down to grab it but Aunt Bella was already there. It was Maisie's wallet, stuffed full of cash. Aunt Bella was holding it up, transfixed.

Maisie's eyes widened and she snatched the wallet back. Aunt Bella kept her hand held there, staring at the space where the wallet had been. She was trembling. Maisie grabbed Simon's arm and hauled him to his feet.

'Right, Simon. Let's head off now. Don't want to impose.'

They were out in the hallway when Aunt Bella's voice cried out.

'You kept it?'

Simon could hear tears in her voice. Maisie was tugging his arm.

'Let's go, Simon.'

'Maisie, what's happening?'

'Nothing. Let's go.'

Aunt Bella appeared in the doorway, tears streaming down her cheeks.

'You bitch!'

Simon was so shocked he froze. Aunt Bella had put every fibre of her being into the insult. She was visibly shaking.

'You *dare* come into this house with *his* wallet?'

'Whose wallet? Maisie what is this?'

'Let's go.'

'THAT'S RIGHT, RUN AWAY. KEEP RUNNING FROM WHAT YOU'VE DONE.'

'Simon, come on.'

'YOU STILL HAVEN'T TOLD HIM?'

'Told me what?'

'Simon…'

'TELL HIM. TELL WHOSE WALLET THAT IS. TELL HIM WHO WENT OUT ON THE CLIFFS LOOKING FOR IT. TELL HIM WHO FELL INTO THE SEA LOOKING FOR *THAT* WALLET.'

'Maisie, what have you done?'

Maisie was struggling with the latch. She was shaking too. Her eyes were starting to leak.

'YOU KEPT IT?'

The door opened and Maisie ran out.

'YOU HAD IT THE WHOLE TIME?'

But Maisie was gone. All that remained was a dark rectangle of the night with the faint echo of running footsteps. Simon stared into it as his aunt collapsed on the floor sobbing behind him. A picture of Huw watched them, smiling, from the dresser.

***

Simon didn't remember going up to bed. He didn't remember anything really. All he knew was that he was sat on his bed staring at the walkie-talkie lying harmlessly on the pillow. Aunt Bella's crying had subsided a few minutes ago. He checked the clock. It was almost midnight.

The house was dark. The wind that Simon was so used to hearing rustling through the trees was gone. Only the sound of blood in his ears remained. The pictures of Huw stared at him from every direction, silent. He looked back at them before getting up from his mattress and taking each and every one down off the wall. He piled the pictures neatly on the floor by the door to his room, face down.

Something flared up in his chest and he snatched the walkie-talkie up off the bed. He took in a deep breath and was just about to start yelling into it when the fight left him. Only emptiness remained. The same emptiness that filled the entire house.

Why hadn't she just told him? Fuck that, why did she have Huw's wallet in the first place? There's no way she actually stole it. Surely.

But he couldn't convince himself. This was the same girl who he'd been spending the past couple of weeks with, stealing from everyone in town. They'd always found excuses to justify it to themselves but they couldn't escape the truth of it. They were thieves. Simple as that. But there's no way she could've stolen Huw's wallet. Maisie wouldn't do that, would she?

Again, Simon put his finger on the walkie-talkie button. He could just ask for clarification right? Maybe Aunt Bella was overreacting. Maybe it wasn't *the* wallet but just a similar one. An honest mistake. Maybe it was all just a misunderstanding. Maybe it wasn't.

Simon dropped the walkie-talkie and fell back onto the duvet. He sank into it. He wished it would submerge him completely and take him deep into a dream where Maisie was normal and Aunt Bella was happy. Actually, he just wanted to dream himself back home.

For the first time in weeks Simon craved his phone. Something mindless to look at, something to give him good news and pictures of happy lives. He wanted to call his mum, to text his friends. His real friends, the ones from home who didn't steal things or wear ugly jumpers or make his family cry. The kind of friends who he had a proper connection with. Friends like...

But no names came to mind. Just a nagging little whispered one from somewhere near the back of his head.

Simon kicked himself free from his bedding and got up, pacing back and forth. He could get about five steps in each direction before having to turn back. The movement helped though. If he just focused on each step then he could cut off the monologue in his head before it got too much momentum.

Simon paced back and forth until his legs got tired. He got into bed and lay awake for most of the night. When he did sleep, it brought him dreams of wandering out on the cliffs alone. He was staggering around in the darkness. He could hear the black waters crashing somewhere beneath him. Then the ground beneath him gave way and he plunged into the abyss.

Chapter 11

It was the first day of summer. Unfortunately, it came a couple of months too early. No one was quite ready for it. All of the clouds that had been blanketing the town slid off the edge of the horizon leaving space for the sun to stretch out. But as Simon sat on the cliff edge he realised there was something wrong. There was no breeze to tickle the grass around him. The wind was gone. The headstones sat undisturbed.

The walkie-talkie perched next to him on a rock. These past few days he'd been taking it with him everywhere he went, not that he'd gone anywhere in particular. Most of the time he'd just come and sat out here. The graveyard shone in the summer's glow. It wouldn't be long before he'd have to mow the grass again.

He couldn't have done it that long ago but after everything that had happened Simon felt like he'd been stuck in this town for years. If it had been suffocating before it was on the verge of choking him now. There was no avenue of escape anymore. No jobs for him to work, no adventures to fill his days. No friends to talk to.

He was well and truly alone out here with no chance to get out and no one to take his mind off it. Not anymore. He heard a tree rustle in the wind somewhere off to his left but the gust didn't make it over to where he sat. He was sweltering in the sun.

He could try praying. He was ashamed to admit how long it had been since he'd tried that. Simon closed his eyes and lay back on the grass allowing his mind to slow down a bit before he started whispering.

'Dear Lord Jesus, I um…'

He what? What did he even have to say at this point?

'God, what do I do? Seriously, what do You want from me? Why did You bring me here? Why did You have to dig up all of Huw's past like that? It's not fair. I was happy at home until You kicked me out and sent me here. Then just as I was starting to like it here You go and ruin everything again. What have I done wrong?'

Nothing.

'Exactly. Aunt Bella's been a mess these last few days. Uncle Aled's not saying anything. Maisie's…'

Go on?

'Maisie's…'

But the words never came. He suddenly remembered Aunt Bella stood on the beach next to him on his very first morning here. Maybe the words to describe that girl just didn't exist.

'You know what? I've got my prayer. I pray that I don't see her again. Think You can do that for me? Just keep her out of my way until mum takes pity on me and let's me go home.'

Would she do that though? Would she just let him leave like that? He reckoned he'd proven that he could be an adult. He'd definitely learned a lesson or two about trusting people, that was for sure. Every night for the past few days Simon had sat by the landline in the front room staring at the wall.

What was he supposed to say to his mum? She'd known the whole time how stupid he was being. Even from all the way in London she'd understand how bad his decisions were. Selling jumpers with this Maisie girl? What a ridiculous idea. Of course it had all gone wrong. What could he say? Sorry mum, I was wrong, you were right. Now can I please just come home?

But, every time he'd picked up the phone, something - pride probably - got in the way. Until he could face up to the fact that he'd failed he was stuck here. And he was was too much of a wuss to even do that.

He'd been tearing up grass without even realising it. There were patches of bare earth on each side of him. His fingers were smeared green. Another memory swam across his mind. He was on his hands and knees chasing the bank notes Maisie had thrown at him before they disappeared off the edge of the cliff. It was this same spot.

Well, if that's what it took to get home then that's what he would do. For the first time in days he thought about the supermarket again. What did he need Maisie for anyway? *He* was the one that came up with all of the good ideas, not her. He knew where the safe was. He could do the heist all by himself. That would show his mum. That would show Maisie.

The fete was coming up fast though. How many days did he have left? It was Sunday so…

Wait. It was Sunday.

Simon groaned. The one thing he'd not wanted to do was skip church. Not for Aunt Bella's sake but for his own. Church was the only thing keeping him sane and here he was sat on the cliff ignoring it. If he ran down he still might be able to make it.

Simon got up and brushed himself off. Just before he ran off he realised that he hadn't closed off his prayer. He couldn't remember where he'd got up to but he figured God heard it all anyway.

'Um, yeah. Amen.'

And with that he was off down the path back into town.

***

The doors to the church opened just as Simon rounded the corner. A tentative old couple stepped out and made their way down the steps arm in arm. They beamed warmly as he stood there panting. The man poked his cane in Simon's direction.

'Afraid you're a bit late there lad.'

'Yeah, I know.'

'Something wrong?'

'No, I just uh… you know. A lot on my mind right now.'

'Hm.'

The couple stopped in front of him. Their heads only came up to his chin. He peered over them into the open doors. He could just about make out Aunt Bella talking to the vicar. The old lady touched his arm softly but Simon was so distracted he almost jumped out of his skin.

'Oh, sorry dear. Didn't mean to give you such a fright.'

'No, no. It's fine.'

'You know, you should go in there and talk to her.'

'Yeah, that's why I came. Aunt Bella's been so-'

'No, no. Not Bella. Maisie.'

'Oh.'

'I don't mean to pry, dear, but ever since the pair of you started spending time together she's really blossomed.'

'Um…'

'Like I said, I don't mean to pry, but the poor dab's sat in there looking like her flock's all in the sea.'

'Right.'

'Anyway, we'd best be off.'

The old lady squeezed his arm again and led her husband off down the lane. They didn't look like they were talking. Simon guessed when you've been with one person for that long words can't be all that necessary. He turned back to the little church.

No one else was coming out so he supposed it was on him to go in. He could just ignore Maisie. She'd probably left already. If not she'd be sat in her usual seat. He could just walk straight in keeping his eyes front and centre. That would work, right? She'd probably see him come in and head out. Yeah, he'd do that.

But just as Simon reached the door, Maisie appeared in it. Both of them immediately looked at the floor. Simon stepped aside for Maisie to come out but she stepped aside for him to go in. Simon waited for a split second then made to go inside just as she tried to step out. They stopped again. He could see her picking at the sleeve of her jumper again. He stood his ground outside.

'You first.'

Maisie made a little sound and hopped down out of the doorway. She didn't look at Simon as she rushed past him but a gust of wind appeared just in time to whip her hair against his cheek. She had a smell. He didn't realise it before but he could smell it now. She smelled kind of like home.

But then she was gone. For a crazy moment Simon was about to call out after her. What would he possibly say? Nothing. There was nothing to say. As soon as she was out of sight he felt that cold resentment creeping back into his chest. He slipped through the doors.

Aunt Bella saw him coming and before Simon could say a word she was crushing him in a hug. For a moment he wasn't quite sure what to do. He still felt a bit awkward around her, particularly after what had happened at dinner but when he felt her slightly uneven breathing he melted and put his arms around her.

For the first time he was struck by just how fragile she was. As a child, every adult looks invincible but now that Aunt Bella was half a foot shorter than him she felt delicate in his arms. If he squeezed her too tightly she might just snap and crumble away forever. Uncle Aled laid a heavy hand on Simon's shoulder. Even his face was showing its age. The sea had worn lines and creases into him like the cracks into the cliffs they lived between.

None of them said anything as they stood there together in the church. Everyone else gave them space and pretended they hadn't noticed anything. After a few minutes the rest of the congregation filtered out. Simon realised it was the first time he'd touched either his aunt or uncle since before dinner with Maisie.

Aunt Bella sniffled as she pulled back from the hug. Uncle Aled had a handkerchief at the ready for her. She tried her best to dry her eyes and nose. For a moment Simon almost apologised for not coming to church but as they stood there in the emptying hall the apology died on his lips. It wasn't necessary. Aunt Bella took in a shaky breath and smiled up at Simon, a proper smile, the first he'd seen from her in days.

'Can we take a walk, sweetie?'

'Sure.'

'I know that lunch is in the oven but we can let it burn a little.'

'I'm sure it'll taste amazing anyway.'

Aunt Bella flapped the wet handkerchief at him, trying to look modest. He felt a warmth coming back into him as they linked arms and walked out of the church.

When Simon had gone inside it had been a hot day. Now it was a beautiful one.

***

They walked slowly along the coastal path, taking breaks at the top of every hill. Simon was happy to go slower than his usual pace. He'd got so used to walking at a hurricane speed with Maisie that it felt nice to accommodate for a couple of slower walkers for once. He actually noticed a lot of little details in the rocks and cliffs that he'd never spotted before. Aunt Bella kept her arm locked around his the whole time.

It didn't take Simon long to figure out where they were heading. The little white walled graveyard where he'd been sat all morning. The headstones poked into view. He spotted something dark perched on a rock where he'd been lying. The walkie-talkie. But they walked past it. Uncle Aled pushed open the little gate to the graveyard and they walked in, single file. Uncle Aled. Then Simon. Then Aunt Bella.

The sea was staggering. All three of them stopped to look at it shimmering at them from where the fourth wall should have been. They could hear the wind somewhere far away from them but here it was still. Huw's headstone had a glow of its own.

Aunt Bella drifted over to it and placed a soft hand on the warm stone. After a moment of staring at the view a little while longer Simon and Uncle Aled joined her. Aunt Bella took Simon's hand in her free one and gave it a little squeeze.

'It isn't a bad spot to leave your boy is it?'

Simon opened his mouth to reply but no words came. He squeezed Aunt Bella's hand back instead. Uncle Aled filled the silence.

'He was good.'

'That he was.'

Aunt Bella shuffled her feet a little and took a little moment before continuing.

'But... what's past is past. We had a good time with our boy but now it's time for us to have a good time with you.'

'I'm sorry I wasn't at church.'

'Oh hush, you live your own life. No one else's.'

'What did I miss?'

'A lot of tears. It was... do you know Corrie ten Boom?'

'I don't think so.'

'During the Second World War she and her family hid a great many jews in their house. They were not jewish themselves. Before long she was arrested and... well you know what being arrested by the Nazis meant. But after her release, much later in her life, she came across one of Nazi officers from the camp where she was held.'

Aunt Bella took a moment to stare out across the sea.

'And she forgave him. Not by herself, she was too heartbroken to do that. She prayed and prayed and God gave her the strength to shake the man's hand.'

She didn't say any more.

The wind whispered something as it went past. After a while longer in the graveyard the three of them returned home to eat their slightly burnt Sunday lunch.

Simon picked up the walkie-talkie on his way out.

***

For most of that week, Simon stayed at home. Aunt Bella would be in and out all day every day as usual, going to yoga, bingo, seeing friends, and having afternoon tea. She'd invite Simon along to everything but for the first time he felt he could actually say no to her. Whenever he did she'd just give him a warm smile and tell him to enjoy his day anyway.

Honestly though, he was still struggling to enjoy himself that much. He'd started reading a lot of books. Sat at home without a phone there wasn't much else to do. He'd given a few half-hearted attempts to find jobs online but if there'd been little out there before then it was a wasteland now. There wasn't a single advertised vacancy within an hour's drive of the house.

So he'd taken to sitting on the sofa and in his room reading. Aunt Bella and Uncle Aled hardly had the most riveting selection. Every single one of his aunt's books had the same front cover: a watercolour painting of an aristocrat woman standing in a country field surrounded by flowers. The field and the women would vary but the content of every book was virtually identical.

On Uncle Aled's side, there were three fiction books and everything else fell into the category of some kind of fishing guide. Not fancying they'd be all that entertaining Simon had read through the rather limited fiction selection:

Moby Dick, Salmon Fishing in the Yemen, and The Old Man and the Sea. He was pleasantly surprised at how fast he was getting through them with so little else to do.

That Thursday, however, Uncle Aled stepped in. Simon had been sat on the sofa since he'd first got up, leaving it only for breakfast, lunch and dinner. He was just getting to the end of Hemingway and starting to wonder which period romance would be most up his street when his uncle's shadow blocked out the light coming from the lamp behind his head. Simon turned to see the old man looking down at him, brow slightly furrowed.

'Good book?'

'Yeah, it's great actually. I don't really want to finish it to be honest.'

'Hm.'

'You really like fishing, don't you?'

Uncle Aled gave him a confused look.

'All your books, they're about fish. You know, Moby Dick, Old Man and the Sea, Salmon Fishing in the Yemen? A bit of a theme.'

'Huh.'

'They're good though.'

'Yes.'

Uncle Aled stayed between Simon and his reading light. Simon raised his eyebrows expectantly. He only had a couple dozen pages left and he was right in the middle of a really important bit. Uncle Aled, as usual, took his time thinking about what he wanted to say. So much so that Simon was just lifting the book back up to continue reading when his uncle interrupted him.

'Come fishing.'

'I'm sorry?'

'Tomorrow.'

'What, with you?'

Uncle Aled nodded. It wasn't up for discussion.

'Um, sure. I guess. I've never been fishing before so… I guess I don't have the right clothes.'

Uncle Aled was already walking out of the room though. He came back in a minute or so later with a stack of wools and waterproofs. He dumped them unceremoniously on Simon's lap. They weighed a tonne.

'Oh jeez, okay. Cool, sure. I'll come fishing tomorrow. Just don't expect me to catch anything.'

Uncle Aled gave him a dry smile. He didn't.

***

Simon came out of his sleep early. He'd definitely been dreaming about *something* but as soon as he opened his eyes it all dissolved under the cold early morning light. The knock that had come from his door was heavier than usual, more of a thud than a knock. It didn't take him long to figure out who was on the other side.

'I'm uh… I'm awake don't...'

A yawn interrupted him. 6am.

'Don't worry. I'll just have quick shower then I'll be ready.'

'Don't shower.'

Uncle Aled's voice filled the room.

'Um, sure. Alright. I'll uh, just get dressed then.'

'Breakfast.'

'And have breakfast.'

Simon looked at the stack of clothes at the foot of his bed. He'd be drowning in layers long before he fell out of the boat he reckoned. It had been sunny the other day, surely he wouldn't need that many clothes. But as Simon thought about it, he realised that he hadn't actually left the house since Sunday. Five days ago. Echoes of the arguments he'd had with his mum when he'd been living at home sounded from the back of his head.

He ignored them and got dressed.

***

Out in the middle of the ocean it was hard to believe that those cliffs could kill anyone. It wasn't that they looked particularly small, they just looked so peaceful. The jagged grey rocks were all topped with a green fuzz. The tide had gone out since Simon and Aled had left exposing little pockets of sand all along the coast that Simon had never seen before from atop the cliffs. There were a thousand tiny beaches, big enough for only two or three people, that would never see a picnic blanket unless one washed up covered in seaweed one day.

Whatever illusions Simon had had about the choice of outfit, he was certainly glad to have so many layers on now. Away from the headlands there was nothing between himself and the sea winds other than a cold spray of water. Another wave hit the side of the boat. Simon had hoped they'd be casting a net to haul in a whole school of fish like in Finding Nemo but instead Uncle Aled had handed him a rod, bait already attached.

Uncle Aled hadn't said a word all day. When he wanted something from Simon he'd point at it, otherwise he did everything himself. Simon felt like a little boy "helping" his dad fix the car. Uncle Aled had prepared the boat, started the motor, unmoored, kicked off, driven them all the way out here, dropped anchor, and prepared both rods for fishing. Simon was starting to wonder why he'd even been brought along at all.

It was an overcast day. All hope of the early summer they'd been teased with was gone. It was back to their regularly scheduled programming: clouds and sea mist. Simon stared off at the cliffs. For a while he'd been watching his line as it bobbed up and down in time with the waves, always a split second behind the boat's own rise and fall, but it was yet to go under the surface. Or at least, as far he could tell. He'd hardly glanced at it this last half hour.

Uncle Aled had very quietly reeled in six fish already. A couple were pretty small but the most recent was the length of his arm and a good few times wider. Simon didn't know enough about fish to even guess what species they were so he thought it best not to open his mouth. Fishing was a pretty self-explanatory activity anyway, probably why Uncle Aled liked it so much. You didn't need to announce that you'd caught a large fish, or what species it was, or what you would do with it. All of that stuff was pretty obvious. You would just cast out your line and fish.

Simon's legs were aching. His sleeves were damp. The walkie-talkie was digging uncomfortably into his leg. His fingers had gone completely numb from the wind chill a long time ago. He could see his whole world from where he sat: his town tucked in the valley by the estuary with its church, pub, hairdressers, and his little home; the bigger town further along the coast with its supermarket, beach, school, and bookshop; then, in the other direction, the little beach he and Maisie would steal crabs, the graveyard beyond that, and beyond that the farm with the caravan that he could just about spy from his window. All his world was in front of his eyes. About a week ago he'd thought that he'd found his place in it, his own little nook.

Now all he could see was what he saw when he'd first arrived: one big stretch of nothing.

There was a wet thud next to him. Uncle Aled had reeled in another fish. It was flapping around dangling from his line, occasionally hitting the side of the boat. It was almost as big as the last. Simon bit his lip and looked back at his own line. Nothing. The bait had probably been eaten off it hours ago. He took a swig of water from the bottle next to him. Uncle Aled had disappeared over to the steering wheel, he was fiddling with the radio or something.

Simon couldn't figure out what this was supposed to be. Was it a bonding exercise? If so then Uncle Aled wasn't doing a great job opening up to him. Maybe it was supposed to be teaching him some kind of lesson. About hard work perhaps? Again, it wasn't really working. Or maybe Uncle Aled was just getting sick of seeing him lying on the sofa. That was probably the most likely. It left a bitter taste in Simon's mouth. He was supposed to be here to get away from his mum, he didn't want to get another person on his case nagging him to do stuff. What was there to do in this town anyway? Fishing? Brilliant, he'd substituted sitting around reading in one place to sitting around feeling cold, staring at a patch of water in another.

Uncle Aled sat back down next to him, busying himself with putting fresh bait on his line. Simon looked across expectantly. If there was a lesson he was being taught here he was all ears but Uncle Aled just nodded back at him before standing up and casting the line out a good five meters further than Simon's. Still no nibble.

At a guess, it was mid-afternoon. The sun was started to get warmer in colour if not in temperature. The cliffs were beginning to glow slightly. That meant they'd only be out here a little while longer surely. They definitely wouldn't stay out after dark, right? But as Simon looked across at Uncle Aled and saw the man sat there so incredibly still he couldn't help but wonder if they'd ever go back to shore or just end up sitting here forever.

Simon tried again to unpack what Aunt Bella had been trying to say to him on Sunday. He'd done a quick search for Corrie ten Boom on their computer. Or at least, as quick of a search as he could do on that machine. As far as he could tell, there was only one thing that Aunt Bella could have meant bringing the story up like she had. She'd forgiven Maisie. Or at least, she was working on it. That was good for her but he it didn't change anything for him. While Simon had forgotten the prayer he'd prayed on Sunday, the sentiment still remained. If he never saw Maisie again, he wouldn't particularly care. He repeated it to himself a few times as he gazed at the cliffs. He wondered where she was out there.

There was another heavier thud next to him. Great. Uncle Aled must have caught an even bigger fish. Then another thud and another. Simon ignored them all, staring at the cliffs still trying to remember where his train of thought had taken him. The thudding, however, continued. Simon sighed and turned to see what kind of fish would be making that kind of racket.

Except there wasn't a fish at all. The thumping sound was coming from his uncle sprawled on the floor on the boat. His eyes were wide and frantic. His hands were clawing at his chest through his raincoat. His breathing was all wrong. He threw out a hand to Simon.

'Oh shit. Oh *shit*, are you okay?'

Uncle Aled rolled onto his back and started writhing around, clenching and unclenching his fists. Simon threw his rod aside and rushed over to his uncle almost toppling over as the boat rocked violently under him.

'Oh shit. Shit. What do I do? What's wrong? Your chest? Your heart? You heart, okay. Is it a heart attack? Hey, don't close your eyes. Keep looking at me. Uncle Aled? Come on, look at me.'

But it was no use. His uncle's eyes were drifting this way and that, barely staying open for more than a few seconds at a time.

'Oh shit. Oh God. Um, okay. Right. Ambulance. No. Coastguard. Coastguard, right.'

Except he didn't have phone. Only a fat, useless walkie-talkie. The radio! The one in the boat. Simon gently laid his uncle down and moved towards the radio Uncle Aled had been fiddling with just a couple of minutes earlier. Wait, recovery position! He turned back and after a bit of effort managed to roll his uncle onto his side. He couldn't remember entirely how to do the arms but it looked good enough. A wave rocked the boat and tipped Uncle Aled onto his back again.

'Oh fuck!'

Simon stumbled over to the radio and pressed down the button.

'Hello? Is anyone out there? My uncle's... he's... I don't know what's wrong with him but he's unconscious. I think he's breathing but it's not good. Is there anyone out there?'

He let go of the button and waited. The world was silent. No one cared.

'Hello?'

Nothing.

'HELLO!'

But no one answered. Simon yanked the cord on the engine but it just sputtered weakly at him. He tried again, feeling tears pricking his eyes, but no matter how hard he pulled it refused to start. Uncle Aled still wasn't moving. His chest was moving up and down but barely. Simon dropped to his knees next to his uncle and bent down to feel his forehead. He felt cold but he probably would feel cold wouldn't he having been in the wind all day?

Something hard was cutting into his side. The walkie-talkie. Without a second thought, Simon grabbed it and pressed the button.

'Maisie. Maisie, listen. I... I need you. Alright? My uncle, he's – shit, I don't know. Look I need your help. Please, *please* listen to me. I'm sorry, alright? For everything. Whatever. It's not important anymore. Look, I need you to help me now. Please answer. Please, Maisie. *I'm sorry!*'

There was a noise beneath him. Uncle Aled's chest was rising and falling faster than before. There was low sound coming from him. A kind of booming rhythmic... laugh. He was laughing. His eyes snapped open and any trace of pain vanished from his face. He grabbed Simon's shoulder and pulled himself up, wiping a tear away from his eye. His laughter seemed to shake the whole boat.

'What the hell was that?'

But Uncle Aled just kept laughing. Simon gaped at him. That just made his uncle laugh even harder. Simon could almost hear the sound echoing off the cliffs back at them. The walkie-talkie crackled into life suddenly and Uncle Aled managed to silence himself for long enough to listen.

'Simon? Hello? What's wrong? Where are you?'

Uncle Aled broke into fresh laughter. Simon gritted his teeth. No way was he responding to Maisie.

'Simon? Do you need an ambulance? I'm calling you an ambulance, okay?'

Damn it. He pressed the button to talk back.

'Don't call an ambulance. It's, uh... don't need an ambulance.'

'What's wrong, Simon? You're scaring the hell out of me, what's happening? Where are you? I'm gonna come and help you.'

'No, no. Don't. It was a, uh… a misunderstanding.'

There was a pause from the other end.

'A misunderstanding?'

'Yeah. Don't worry, it's all fine. Sorry for calling you or whatever.'

'You're not messing with me, are you?'

'No. I'm sorry.'

'Don't apologise. If there's an emergency, call me. Okay? You don't have to speak to me any other times or like me or anything. Just, if you need help… you know. I'm here.'

'Yeah. Um, thanks.'

'Mhm.'

Uncle Aled had stopped laughing. He was raising his eyebrows at Simon.

'What?'

But his uncle just raised them even further.

'*What?* What else was I supposed to do? The radio wasn't working and the engine didn't start.'

Uncle Aled grinned, got up and went round to the radio. He flipped the switch back on. Then he bent down to the engine and a slid a little piece out of his pocket and back into place.

'Seriously? You planned that whole thing just to get me to talk to her?'

Uncle Aled shrugged.

'Well, congrats. You gave me the biggest scare of my life. I hope you're happy. Aunt Bella's gonna be furious when she finds out though.'

***

As it turned out though, Aunt Bella wasn't furious. In fact, it took her even longer to stop laughing than it had taken Uncle Aled. She had two solid streams running down each cheek before she managed to get a hold of herself. Uncle Aled was sat across the table at dinner acting out Simon's reaction in the biggest show of drama Simon had ever seen him give. All he while he just stared down at his mash. Even he was starting to see the funny side.

'Oh Simon, you poor love.'

Then Aunt Bella was giggling again. He had to admit, it was nice to have a bit of laughter back in the house after the week they'd had. He just wished that it wasn't at his expense. Not even that actually, he just wished that it hadn't taken his uncle faking his own heart attack to bring it out.

'So how was your first fishing lesson then?'

Simon smiled dryly.

'Honestly, I'm not sure it's for me.'

Uncle Aled chuckled and squeezed Simon's shoulder. Simon had to give his uncle some credit at least. He hadn't repeated any of the swearing or, more importantly, the bit when Simon called Maisie on the walkie-talkie. As far as Aunt Bella knew, it was just a harmless prank. The squeeze on his shoulder told Simon that he didn't have to worry about his aunt finding any of this out either. He relaxed a little lower in his chair and allowed himself to smile properly.

Still, it was Friday night and, whether he liked it or not, he would have to see Maisie on Sunday. What was he supposed to say to her then? Sorry for the false alarm? Was he even supposed to say anything at all? As much as he didn't want to admit it, the sincerity in her voice when she told him to call her if he was ever in trouble was...

It was nothing. No matter what his aunt and uncle felt about Maisie, he sure as hell wasn't so ready to forgive her for everything. It was nice to hear her voice again though. No, it wasn't. He set his fork down as he swallowed his last mouthful. His aunt and uncle had barely touched their meals from all the laughter.

'Thanks for dinner. It was delicious.'

'Oh, you say that every time, sweetie.'

'Well, that's because it's true every time. I'm gonna head up if that's alright.'

'Of course it is, dear. Make sure you say goodnight before bed though.'

Aunt Bella brushed his arm as he walked past. She was still struggling to contain her laughter.

Chapter 12

Simon was dreading Sunday more than any other day he could remember. Even his first day of school couldn't have been that bad right? All of his Saturday was spent staring at one page of his book. He must have reread the same sentence a hundred times over and it still sounded alien to him. Every time he tried again his brain had drifted back to Maisie before he even reached the first full stop.

Uncle Aled would glance over at him occasionally with a knowing smile on his face. Aunt Bella, oblivious as anything, went about her day with her usual enthusiasm. Simon found himself coasting on autopilot through lunch, dinner and eventually into bed. Before he knew it, it was 2am and he was still wide awake. He chewed his lip and stared at that same spot in the ceiling he now knew better than his own reflection. What did he care about Maisie? What was so special about *her* that he'd been thinking about all day?

He couldn't even remember properly what he'd been thinking. Except that was a lie. He'd been replaying all the time they'd spent together, from start to finish and then back through again. Each time he'd remember something else she'd said and catch himself smiling. He pretended that it hadn't happened every time. She was a thief and that's all she was.

Suddenly the sun was up and Simon was awake. He didn't quite remember falling asleep or waking up but he must have because several hours had passed. For a few seconds he lay there picking apart carefully what were memories and what were dreams. All of them had Maisie in them and he was quick to throw a few of them by the wayside.

Then he was at church. As much as he wanted the morning to drag by, it slipped between his fingers leaving him stood about a foot behind his aunt and uncle before the open wooden doors. Uncle Aled glanced back at him as they stepped inside. The look he gave Simon took him aback. It wasn't the mischievous smile that he'd been wearing for the past few days. It was something Simon couldn't quite describe. It was the same face he'd given Simon when he'd first shaken his hand when they picked him up from the train station. Something lifted from Simon's shoulders.

They'd arrived slightly late and so most of the church was full. To Simon's relief, Maisie wasn't there yet. There was a tap on his shoulder. The vicar was stood smiling behind him.

'Simon, hello.'

'Oh, hey. How's it going?'

'Splendid, my boy. There is a slight issue, however, that I was hoping that you would perhaps be able to help with.'

'Okay?'

'Excellent! Thank you, my boy. I knew you'd be up for it.'

'Sorry, I don't know what *it* is?'

'Well, as you well know the school fete in the next town over is happening this Friday.'

This Friday?

'And well we've run into a spot of bother. Every year the church organises the treasure hunt for all of the children to get involved with but the Pattersons who usually hide all of the eggs have sadly left us.'

'Oh I'm so sorry.'

'Yes, it's most regrettable. They moved to Cardiff to be closer to their son. Anyway, thank you so much for agreeing to help.'

'Oh, I-'

'No need to be so humble! I really appreciate it. There are one hundred eggs to be hidden. It can be difficult to keep track of many more than that. We bought them for Easter but we figure an egg hunt can be an all-seasons event.'

'Right.'

'You sound a bit wary. I assure there's nothing to worry about. You can still go around all the stalls or work your own if need be. Besides you'll have young Maisie to help you out so it shouldn't be too arduous.'

Simon attempted to smile at the news but it probably didn't look all that convincing. He doubted the vicar's eyesight was good enough to distinguish a smile from a grimace these days anyway. The old man shuffled off to the front of the church to start the service. Simon turned to sit with his aunt and uncle near the front but the row was full. Aunt Bella shrugged apologetically at him.

In fact, every pew in the church was full except for the one right at the back. Maisie's pew. Simon was about to see if he could trade places with someone when the vicar started talking from the lectern. He'd missed his chance. At least Maisie wasn't here yet. With any luck she'd be skipping church today. He slid into the pew and fixed his eyes on the front. No sooner had he stopped than Maisie appeared through the door and stopped dead seeing him sat there. She lowered her eyes to the floor quickly. The vicar's wheezing voice was almost loud enough to drown out her whisper.

'I can sit somewhere else if you want.'

But she couldn't. The little church was completely full. Heads were starting to turn in their direction. Simon sighed.

'No, it's fine. Sit here.'

'Are you sure?'

'Yeah. Just sit down.'

Maisie slid into the pew next to him. She sat as far over to the edge as possible, leaving about a foot of space between them. Simon caught himself watching her out of the corner of his eye. She was constantly picking at her sleeve. He'd never seen her looking so small.

They stood for the first hymn. Simon hadn't heard the vicar say to do so but noticed when everyone in front of them got to their feet. Simon braced himself for Maisie's singing. It had been a long time since he'd heard it. He could probably ignore her though. But as the Casio organ blared into life and everyone droned the first line there was a noticeable silence next to him.

He glanced across at Maisie. Her hair was hiding most of her face from him but he could just make out her lips. She was mouthing the words, so quietly that he doubted she could even hear herself. Her eyes remained fixed on the floor the whole time. Something in Simon's chest dropped.

The first verse ended. When the second droned into life he waited for her to join in but nothing changed. She just kept on staring at the stone floor under her feet, lips tracing the outlines of the words. Simon gripped the pew in front and cleared his throat. This was a dumb idea.

The third verse started and with it Simon burst into song. He couldn't remember ever having sung this loud. The old couple in front of him actually jumped and turned back to look at him in surprise. Out of the corner of his eye Simon saw Maisie tilt her head in his direction slightly. With every word he raised his volume until he was pretty sure he was drowning out the rest of the congregation. A few heads turned back to look at him and he felt his face burn but pushed on nonetheless singing louder and louder.

There was a high note coming up and Simon took in a deep breath to hit it. His voice cracked and he completely missed the note. The couple in front of him tutted audibly and turned back to give him angry looks. Simon glanced across at Maisie. Just beneath her hair he could see a little smile playing around on her lips. The verse ended and Simon paused to catch his breath. Just one more verse of embarrassment to get through before it was over. He wasn't sure he'd be allowed back in after this.

But when the verse started another voice joined his own. It was quiet at first, especially compared to him, but it was there. A pure little sound, gliding smoothly over the surface of all of the other voices in the room. Simon messed up the words and the voice faltered slightly to hide a giggle but when it came back it was stronger than before. As the verse went on Maisie's voice slowly swelled louder and louder, growing more confident with each line. She was almost back to her usual volume when the song ended and everyone sat down.

Now there were a lot of disapproving looks thrown Simon's way. He spied Uncle Aled giving him a wink between a sea of heads. He thought he just about made out the soft boom of his uncle's chuckle over the sounds of pews being filled. Simon stole a glance in Maisie's direction but she was looking pointedly the other way.

Wait, he was supposed to be annoyed at her. He crossed his arms and immediately felt like a little kid. He uncrossed them and suddenly noticed just how awkward his arms were. Where did he normally put them? By his sides? On his lap? They all felt weird now. He brushed against Maisie's arm accidentally and jumped making the pew squeak. He made a couple of fists and placed them on his knees. That definitely wasn't right but it would do for now.

The rest of the service kind of passed in an awkward blur. Simon spent as much time as possible trying to figure out where he normally put his arms to avoid thinking about Maisie. It was kind of difficult with her ugly colourful jumper filling up the edge of his vision. They sang a few more hymns but Simon didn't try his luck again. Maisie was singing again, if a little quietly, and that was all that mattered. What was he thinking? Why did he care if she sang or not? Why was he even thinking about her?

Then the service was over. Simon froze. He hadn't planned for this. Why hadn't he planned for this? What was he supposed to do? He could just leave. That would work. Maybe say 'excuse me' as he went past and be out of there. That was a shout actually. Unless Aunt Bella and Uncle Aled wanted to stick around. Or he could wait. Maybe Maisie would leave first. He could just sit here and-

There was a tap on his shoulder. It was so tentative he might have missed it entirely if he wasn't so on edge already. He turned to see Maisie half looking at him. She was fiddling with her sleeve again. Simon decided to look at that instead of her face. The hem was coming apart. When Maisie spoke it was in a voice so quiet that he had to lean over just to hear it.

'Um, Simon. If you don't want to talk to me that's fine. I understand. It's not your fault. I'm used to it. Not that you should worry about me. I... Sorry. Um, I just wanted to apologise for not telling you about everything. Um, but yeah. I'll leave now, I don't... you don't have to talk to me.'

She got up quickly and rushed towards the door. Simon's hand caught her arm. He hadn't meant to stop her. His mouth opened to start speaking before he knew what he was going to say.

'I'm sorry too.'

'No, you ain't done nothing wrong. It's my fault. Don't apologise.'

'Maisie, wait. I... I don't understand.'

He let go of her arm. He half expected her to run out of the church but she stood there nervously for a moment. Then she sat back down next to him.

The rest of the church was emptying out. They sat for long time without saying anything. By the time Maisie spoke there was only the vicar left in the church and he had the decency to pretend to be sweeping something up all the way over in the opposite corner.

'Simon. I've never told anyone what happened.'

'You don't have to.'

'I want to but only if you want to hear it. I've been keeping it a secret for five years, I can keep it for longer.'

'I just want to know why you have his wallet.'

Maisie took in a shaky breath and looked up at the ceiling. She gathered her thoughts before she started talking.

'Dad and Huw were best mates. But sometimes best mates don't tell each other everything. Huw had… issues. Not just with drinking but with, I don't know, himself I guess. He didn't talk about it with anyone. I was always in the pub with dad and I was usually the only sober one in there. I saw Huw's face when he thought no one else was looking. He liked me. Said he used to be the only black sheep in town but together we made two.'

Maisie paused. The vicar disappeared into a side room leaving them alone together in the hall.

'Every night he'd give me his wallet to look after. I think it was to stop him drinking too much. But, um, one night – *the* night – he didn't look so drunk when he gave me the wallet. Told me to keep hold of it, not let it out of my sight, until I saw him again. I didn't really know what he meant. Then, when everyone else was smashed, he got up, walked over to the door and left. The last time I saw him he was holding a finger up to his lips. I laughed because I thought he was messing round. His eyes looked kinda sad though.'

'Maisie…'

'They say the cliff fell in but we all knew that spot was loose already. It wouldn't'a taken much to make it give way.'

Maisie's voice cracked and she stopped talking. Simon put a hand on her shoulder. He could feel her trembling. When she spoke though, her voice was clear.

'I don't care if you believe me or not. I just want you to know that's how it happened okay?'

'I believe you.'

Maisie managed to hold it together for a few seconds but then she crumbled. Her face fell into her hands and sobs filled the church. Simon hesitated then put his arm around her. They sat together on that uncomfortable pew for a long time.

***

Simon didn't go home for lunch. He was sure his aunt and uncle would understand. Instead he walked along the coastal path with Maisie. They didn't really say anything to each other. They didn't have to. All the while Simon was thinking of all the moments he'd missed from Maisie's life. She'd lived a full eighteen years before he'd even met her. What else had happened in that time?

He hadn't even realised it was her birthday when they'd first spent the day together. Simon stopped. Maisie looked at him quizzically but he didn't say anything, just smiled slightly.

'What's that look about?'

'Nothing. I've just had a little idea.'

'What?'

'You'll see. Reckon you could meet me on the beach tomorrow?'

'In the morning?'

'No, the evening. Like six, maybe?'

'Um, yeah I guess. Why?'

'Ah, don't worry about it.'

Maisie turned to him.

'Look, Simon. Just because I've told you about, you know, about Huw, it doesn't mean you have to be friends with me or whatever. You don't even have to talk to me anymore. It's fine, I understand.'

'Just come to the beach tomorrow, okay?'

'Alright.'

They kept walking, silence falling once again. It was a good kind of silence. Maybe good was the wrong word for it but Simon couldn't come up with anything better. Everything was slowly starting to feel right again. No, not right. He couldn't figure out what he meant. He walked Maisie all the way along the coastal path, further than he'd ever walked before. Past the crabbing beach. Past the graveyard. All the way to the little farm with the caravan. Maisie stopped.

'This is me.'

'You live here, at the farm? I didn't realise-'

'Not the farm itself. Um...'

Simon's eyes fell on the caravan. It clicked.

'Right.'

'Um, yeah. Thanks for walking me. Dad's probably still asleep so I've gotta be quiet when I go in.'

'Sure. Um, yeah. I'll see you tomorrow.'

'Yeah. For the big mystery surprise.'

Stood there, in front of the caravan, Maisie still looked small. Her voice was still a bit quiet and her eyes still looked downwards a bit. Without thinking, Simon hugged her. She was tense in his arms. Then softened. Her arms crept around his back and her head nestled into his shoulder as if it was always meant to be there. They stayed there for a moment, neither wanting to leave.

Eventually they both let go and walked in opposite directions. A passer-by would have smiled warmly if they'd spotted the two of them in the mid-afternoon light.

Chapter 13

Once again, Simon found himself staring out into the sea. He wondered how many hours he must have spent looking at this exact same view over the past few weeks. Every time he looked at it though he was reminded just how impossible it was to remember. You can see the sea in photographs, you can picture it perfectly in your head, and yet it is only when you actually look at it in person that you remember just what it is that makes it so beautiful.

The clouds had been jostling around in the sky, drawing enormous shadows on the water throughout the day. The tide had come all the way in and was now almost all the way back out again. Simon had to look away as the sun sunk out of the bottom of a cloud. It turned the ocean in front of him a white so brilliant that he had to look at his feet. The shadows they were casting had grown much longer since last he'd checked.

Not for the first time that day Simon's heart was hammering. Everything was ready, it was all perfectly set up, and yet the more he thought about it the more convinced he became that he was making a mistake. It was too late now. Honestly it had been too late pretty much all day. He'd been going here and there in the town spending more money than he could remember having done for a long time. Fortunately, Aaron hadn't been in the supermarket.

5:57pm. It had only been three minutes since he'd last checked. She'd probably be here any minute. There were still a few dog walkers on the beach. A couple of dogs had bounded up to him while he'd been getting everything ready. They just wanted to say hello and have a sniff but their owners called them away, giving Simon expressions of mixed amusement and confusion.

It only occurred to him then that he hadn't planned at all what to do with everything afterwards. It had taken him all day to set this up. If he didn't think of something, he'd be here all night tidying up. He was just trying to figure out exactly what he was supposed to do when a gust of wind blew a grain of sand in his eye. Simon stumbled backwards, cursing to himself. He blinked a few times and wiped away the tears.

When he regained focus Maisie was standing just a few feet away from him. Her hair was blustering this way and that. Her eyes were wide. Her hands were at her mouth. She was staring at Simon as he stood on the picnic blanket under the massive banner.

HAPPY ALMOST BIRTHDAY MAISIE!

He rubbed his eye one more time and waited for Maisie to say something but she just kept staring, hands over her mouth. Giving his best stab at showmanship Simon half raised his hands in the air.

'Surprise?'

Maisie unfroze, screamed and ran to Simon, smothering him in a hug before he could ready himself. They almost stumbled backwards onto the picnic basket. Then as quickly as she'd grabbed him she released him, jumping back to stare at the banner, then Aunt Bella's candle lanterns, the picnic basket, the cake.

'Wait, you made a cake?!'

'I tried my best, okay? Honestly, I wouldn't eat it if I were you.'

But Maisie had already run over to get a closer look. Simon couldn't help but grin. Her reaction was way better than anything he'd been imagining. He turned to watch her as she darted from one thing to the next, a look of ecstatic shock plastered all across her face. He laughed when she jumped up and gave him another, slightly shyer hug.

'You actually did all this for me?'

'Mhm.'

'I... I can't believe it.'

'Well, you didn't get a proper birthday before so it's only fair.'

'But...'

She gestured helplessly at the little setup on the beach. In the fading light Simon had to admit that the little lanterns dotted around the sand had been a nice touch.

'*This*?'

'You deserve it.'

Maisie was about to argue when Simon sat himself down on the picnic blanket, looking out again at the setting sun. After a moment, Maisie joined him. Her head kept swivelling this way and that, trying to take it all in.

'Mate, I don't know what to say.'

'You don't need to say anything. Happy birthday.'

'Thanks. Bit late but thanks.'

'Oh sorry, I'll just pack this all down then. Save it for next year.'

'I mean, it's not *that* impressive.'

'You should see the fireworks.'

'You haven't.'

'Nah, of course I haven't. You're not that big of a deal.'

Maisie punched his shoulder but it wasn't as hard as her usual punches. The sand was now a fiery orange. The clouds were lit up in pinks, purples and yellows above them. Simon looked at them as he spoke.

'I'm sorry about everything.'

'You ain't got nothing to be sorry about.'

'I do. I didn't want to hear you out. You're my friend and I shouldn't have doubted you.'

'I'm not very good at keeping friends.'

'Well, I'm still here. Aren't I?'

'Yeah because you're a nutter, that's why.'

Maisie gestured up at the banner over their heads. Simon grinned.

'Well two's company at least.'

'You're telling me. Now are you gonna open that picnic basket or just sit here twiddling your thumbs forever?'

Simon laughed and opened the basket for her. Inside were sandwiches, pork pies, cocktail sausages, sausage rolls, scotch eggs, salad, cheese and crackers, a bottle of white wine, and a few bars of expensive chocolate. Maisie's eyebrows shot up and her jaw dropped.

'Mate.'

'You're still a meat eater right?'

'*Mate.*'

Simon laughed. Maisie had bypassed the sandwiches and salad straight away and had a whole pork pie in her mouth before Simon could say another word. She swallowed it down and immediately grabbed another handful of food. Gingerly, Simon reached past her for the bottle of wine and pulled it out, trying to remember how waiters presented wines in restaurants. He didn't know the first thing about wine but picked up a fairly expensive bottle and hoped for the best. Maisie put a hand to her mouth and spoke through her food.

'Not gonna lie, I kinda prefer red.'

'Do you actually? I can run up and change it if you want? It's not a big deal.'

'The look on your face! Oh mate, it's like I've got my own little butler. I'm just messing with you, white's fine with me.'

'Hilarious.'

'You did bring glasses right?'

'Yeah, of course. They're right here.'

Simon raised his middle finger. A nearby dog walker tutted loudly. Maisie was struggling not to burst out laughing. A scotch egg tumbled off of her lap and onto the sandy blanket. She was just about to pick it up when a pair of jaws appeared out of nowhere and snatched it away.

Before either of them could do anything, the animal leapt at their picnic basket, scattering food across the sand. The hulking black dog swung its body around and buried its snout in the basket, chomping and slobbering audibly. A woman was shouting, running across the beach to them but by the time she arrived it was too late. All of the picnic that Simon had so lovingly gathered was either coated with sand or in the stomach of the beaming black collie, trying to lick both of their faces.

The owner grabbed the dog's collar and pulled it back. She stood there for a moment apologising profusely but the two young people in front of her were too busy rolling on the ground laughing to reply. After a confused moment, the owner started to laugh too. The collie bounded from person to person barking excitedly at all the food she'd just managed to eat. The dog took some persuading to head off home. She liked her new friends too much and they seemed to like her a lot too. They'd even fed her.

Wiping tears away from his eyes, Simon had a look in the basket. The chocolate bars were still there, as was the salad and a single egg mayo sandwich which looked suspiciously wet. A couple of the lanterns had been kicked over as well in the scuffle. The candles lay on their sides smoking slightly in the sand.

'Happy birthday?'

Maisie giggled, then lay back laughing again. As much as Simon wanted to join in again he couldn't help but do the maths in his head to figure out just how much money he'd spent feeding that dog. On top of that, they had no dinner left to eat. Maisie sat up and peered over his shoulder into the basket.

'Huh. There's not much left.'

'Mhm.'

'It's fine we can eat chocolate.'

'No, it's your birthday meal. We've got to have proper food.'

'No, this is fine. Don't worry.'

Maisie fished out the egg mayo sandwich and even managed a couple of tentative bites before quietly abandoning it in the sand next to her. The seagulls were starting to circle overhead. Simon sighed.

'I'm so sorry. This was supposed to be your party and it's all gone wrong already.'

'Don't be stupid. You've got nothing to be sorry about.'

Simon was about to reply when a flurry of wings filled his vision. A couple of seagulls had started their attack. Simon snapped. He leapt to his feet and kicked out at them. They hopped easily out of harm's way and watched him as he waved his arms yelling, trying to scare them off. Something warm and wet landed on his head and started to dribble down.

Simon froze. He turned to Maisie. She was in the exact same pose she'd been in when she first arrived at the beach, hands at her mouth, eyes wide, staring at the wet spot on the top of his head. She held herself together as best she could but her restraint could only last so long. She collapsed onto the sand, rolling round with tears of laughter in her eyes as Simon felt the warm liquid dribble down towards his neck. The seagulls saw their opportunity and swarmed what little food was left.

***

Maisie was grinning into her fish and chips. She'd at least been courteous enough to suggest they bring their food back down to the picnic blanket to eat. Mercifully the seagulls had moved on but Simon hair was still slightly crusty. Maisie had to stop looking at him entirely otherwise she'd lose it again.

The wind had picked up since they'd gone up to get their fish and chips. Simon could feel himself starting to shiver. He hadn't thought to bring a blanket or anything. He'd almost finished his chips but Maisie's had hardly been touched. Every time she took a bite she had to fight back her giggles.

The sky wasn't full of beautiful colours anymore, it was a deep blue with a couple of hesitant twinkles starting to emerge.

'I might go and wash my hair.'

Maisie laughed into her newspaper full of chips. Simon scowled.

'I'm serious. It's all caked in there.'

But Maisie only laughed harder.

'Has anyone ever told you you've got the worst bedside manner ever? Imagine if this was a funeral, you wouldn't be able to control yourself.'

'Not if you'd died with bird poo in your hair. I'm sorry but if you go out like that then I get a free pass.'

Simon gave a tired smile. He was starting to see the funny side.

'Maisie, I'm sorry about the food.'

'Oh my god, stop apologising! Besides, this fish is great and to be honest, I'd sacrifice a basket of pork pies any day to see your face when the bird dropped that bomb.'

'You weren't the one paying for all that food.'

Maisie sobered up a bit.

'Yeah, I was gonna ask. How much did that cost? I'm happy to split it if you want.'

'No, no. It's your almost birthday. It was a present from me.'

'Still, it musta cost a lot.'

'Oh yeah, I'm properly broke now.'

'Well I reckon I know a way to make a quick bit of money round as it happens.'

Simon didn't reply for a moment. When he did, he voice was deliberate.

'So you still want to go through with it?'

'Fete's this Friday. That gives us four days to figure out what the hell we're doing. Plenty of time for a big noggin like yours.'

'Maisie, are you sure about this?'

'Why? You're not getting cold feet are you?'

Again Simon considered his reply.

'I don't want to risk what would happen if we got caught. There's too much to lose.'

'Ah, don't worry about that. There's a simple fix there.'

Simon smiled dryly.

'We don't get caught?'

'We don't get caught.'

Maisie took another mouthful, made a little noise through the food and sat forward, facing Simon. She swallowed and continued.

'Look, I get why you're nervous. I do, genuinely. But this is our chance. We get the money, we pay back everything we owe, and we fix everything we've done wrong. Fresh start. For both of us.'

'You can sell your jumpers.'

'Exactly.'

'And I can go home.'

Maisie didn't say anything. Simon nodded to himself, gently at first then firmer until he looked up at Maisie. She was peering back at him in the fading light.

'You won't have to live with your dad anymore.'

Maisie nodded back at him.

'Alright, screw it. Let's rob that supermarket.'

Maisie grinned, jumped up to her feet and stretched out a hand to him. Her fish and chips abandoned in the sand. Simon grinned up at her.

'Where are you going?'

'The sea. Wanna come?'

'What, now?'

'Yeah now!'

'It'll be freezing.'

'And?'

'And I'm wearing jeans.'

'Roll 'em up. Come on, live a little.'

And with that Maisie was running off in the direction of the water. It looked as black as the slate cliffs around them. Simon ran a hand through his hair and felt something soft under his fingertips. He almost gagged. He could hear Maisie splashing around in the shallows already. Simon got up, grumbling to himself.

'Fine. But I'm just washing my hand. That's it, I'm just going to wash my hand.'

Two hours later, they traipsed back up the beach. Shivering and soaking wet, the darkness hiding their exhausted grins.

Chapter 14

The sun rose and set. Then did it again and again and, before anyone was quite ready for it, Friday arrived. The first van pulled into the field by the school before the sun had even risen, while the sky was still a pale bluish grey. It swung into place. The headlights died. The driver just sat there inside sipping a black coffee watching the sea.

Ten minutes later, another car arrived. The two sat side by side, looking out over the waters. The sun rose from behind them, casting their shadows all the way along to the fence. Neither car opened their doors for a good half hour. Soon another van joined them and seemed to snap both drivers out of their reveries. At almost the exact same time all three drivers got out.

Aaron watched them all open their boots from across the street. He flicked through the set of keys in hands without taking his eyes off of the figures in the field as they started to set up their various stalls. He tried to put the key into the lock but missed. After a bit of fiddling the doors to the supermarket squeaked open.

He stepped inside. He always liked being here alone before all of the lights came on. Before his employees arrived. Before any customers started emptying the shelves. Whistling a tune he'd come up with himself, he started his daily walk through the aisles. He grabbed a Snickers from the first aisle, a banana from the second, and a yoghurt from the fridge.

A car rumbled past outside, momentarily filling the supermarket with golden beams of light that chased the shadows from one end of the room to the other. Aaron instinctively slid back behind a rack of sunglasses so the beams wouldn't touch him. The car swung into the school's field across the road and joined the other three. It was so quiet inside that he could just about hear the drivers talking to one another from all the way over here.

He licked his moustache and stepped back out of his hiding place. Unwrapping the Snickers and sticking it in his mouth he took off his leather jacket. There was a coat stand behind the counter. He tried to throw his jacket onto it like he did every morning. It missed by a couple of feet and thumped to the floor. He licked his moustache again, walked around behind the tills, and picked the jacket up.

With one last check out of the windows, Aaron got to work. He went along the line of tills, one by one popping each one open. He rifled through the notes in each doing a rough tally of how much money was there. It had been a good week. His moustache curled up at the corners.

He glanced towards the doors again. Clear. Aaron grabbed the stack of twenties out of the first till and slid seven of them into his pocket. He put the stack back and did the same thing with the tens. The next till had less money in it so he only took five of each. Then the next till and the next until Aaron got to the end of the line with a nice bit of cushioning in his back pocket.

Grinning to himself he tried to kick the drawers shut but a couple of them bounced back at him. He missed the last one entirely. With all of the tills properly closed, he took one last look at the door and another out of the window before ducking away into his back office. Again he kept the lights off as he walked in. There was a slice of pizza on his desk from the previous day that he'd forgotten about. Scooping it up, he bent down to the safe, taking one last glance around him to see if the coast was clear, before grabbing the wad of cash out of his back pocket and throwing it in there and slamming the door shut.

Aaron let out a sigh and straightened up. He opened the yoghurt up and dipped his pizza crust into it. A brainwave hit him. He grabbed a crusty brown knife off the side and cut up the banana. He then put the slices on the pizza and then drizzled yoghurt over the top, garnishing with the last few bites of his Snickers bar. He stood there grinning in the darkness finishing off his breakfast.

Only once it was all gone Aaron flipped on the lightswitch. The bulb took a few attempts but eventually got there. He started whistling again, louder this time and strode back out into the store. He stood there proudly surveying his dominion as the tube lights flickered and lit up. There was a smear of yoghurt trapped in his moustache but he didn't notice it.

***

The smear of yoghurt remained in Aaron's moustache all the way through the morning as he stood in the supermarket doorway watching the fete slowly come together. Stalls were assembled, gazebos put up, signs hung on any free surfaces, and Aaron just stood there watching. As far as he was concerned the only thing this fete was good for was getting kids to come in here buying sweets afterwards.

A four-by-four pulled up on the far end of the field. It parked next to come churchy looking stall. Aaron vaguely recognised the old people who got out of the front seats. He'd seen them round the supermarket a few times. He was about to look away when the back doors of the car opened. Even from this distance he could recognise that Simpson boy and, let's be honest, the brat with him was hard to miss in *that* jumper. The boy turned around and somehow spotted him. Jesus, he was waving. The girl joined in.

Aaron's lip curled. What a pair. Before he quite knew what he was doing Aaron strode out of the automatic doors. He was halfway across the road when he remembered to lock them. Couldn't let anyone just walk in there after all. He went back and fiddled with the lock until it clicked. His hands were shaking for some reason.

With what he hoped was a dramatic turn he headed back across those two, fists clenched. They weren't looking at him anymore but were unloading something out of the back of the car. The tarmac under him became grass. It was still a bit wet from the dew. Aaron was so distracted that he caught one of the guy ropes on a gazebo and almost went face first into the mud. Some guy holding a tray of crabs started yelling at him but Aaron stormed on pretending he hadn't heard.

Only a few meters away, he was about to start yelling himself when he heard what the brat girl was saying.

'...the police are your best bet.'

'You think?'

'Yeah. Look, just tell them about the safe.'

Aaron's heart dropped. He looked around wildly for somewhere to hide. There was a stack of boxes between him and them. He dived behind just as they turned round. How they didn't see him he did not know.

'Maisie, I'm just not sure about it. I don't want to be a snitch.'

'He stole money. Like lots of money. *And* he fired you.'

'I mean, I *did* quit.'

'Same thing. Look, there'll be a couple of police officers here. There always are. I say you go up to them and just ask them to look into it.'

'Alright, fine. I'll do it. You don't know when they'll get here do you? Might be better just to get it over and done with before the fete starts.'

'They're always pretty early. To be honest, I'm surprised they're not here already. Give me a hand with this box will you?'

'Sure.'

Aaron listened to their feet walking away. He held his breath for a moment. A woman was giving him a funny look from across the field. He leapt up to his feet and dusted himself down. She kept staring so he gave her a little nod before scarpering back to the supermarket. As he was unlocking the door he licked his moustache nervously. He tasted warm yoghurt mixed with sweat.

He tried to walk calmly through to the shop. There was no one around to see him but it was for his own benefit as much as anything. Past one aisle then the next then the next. Then all of a sudden he was running. If the police were going to be here at any minute he needed to get rid of the money fast. He snatched a roll of bin bags from the counter and crashed through the door into the back office.

It took him three attempts to get into the safe. His hands were shaking so much that he kept missing the buttons. Finally the heavy little door swung open and a cascade of notes slid out onto the floor. There was a noise somewhere close by. A squeaking sound. The doors.

Aaron froze and snapped his head towards the office door. It was slightly ajar, just enough for him to see a figure walking around out there. Fast as he could Aaron started shovelling money into the bin bag. The officers would surely be heading straight for the back office. That's where Simpson would have told them to look. Giving up on grabbing handfuls, Aaron tipped the safe on its side and slid the remaining money into the bag. He managed to tie it shut just as a voice called out from the other side of the door.

'Hello? Anybody around?'

That didn't sound like a police officer. Forgetting the bin bag clenched in his hand Aaron shot over to the door and kicked it open to find Simpson stood there waiting by the till.

'Hey. I was just wondering if I could buy these quickly? I know you aren't open yet but…'

Simpson was holding up a role of masking tape. Aaron tried to catch his breath.

'Sorry, I haven't interrupted anything, have I?'

'No. Of course not.'

'Alright, well can I buy this then?'

Aaron scowled. Simpson spotted the bag in his hand.

'You've started emptying the bins yourself?'

'No… um, yeah.'

'Right.'

Neither of them moved.

'So, can I buy this?'

'We're closed.'

'Seriously?'

'Seriously. Come back in twenty minutes, boy.'

Simpson shoved the tape in his pocket and turned to walk out.

'That's stealing!'

'What are you gonna do about it?'

Aaron was about to charge after him when he remembered the bin bag still clutched in his hand. He looked at Simpson, then back at the bag. Simpson stopped in the doorway, with an eyebrow raised.

'You gonna throw that out or just keep standing there?'

Aaron licked his moustache, gulped, and let out a breath.

'I'm gonna take it out.'

'Let me get the door for you then.'

'Piss off, boy.'

But Simpson had already walked across to the back exit and was holding the door open expectantly. He didn't have much choice.

Aaron tried to give the boy the sourest face he could muster as he walked past and out back. Simpson followed him out, hands in his pockets. Aaron rounded the corner and walked headlong into a hulking figure holding a cigarette. Phil had been waiting out here the whole time. Aaron almost dropped the bag in surprise.

'What the hell are you doin' here?'

Phil just grunted and nodded at the cigarette in his hand.

'When did you get here?'

Phil shrugged.

'Jesus Christ.'

Simpson cleared his throat. Aaron scowled. He really didn't have much choice at all. Hoisting the bag of money up onto his shoulder he lifted one of the big lids open. Juice dribbled onto his shoe. Before he lost his nerve Aaron tipped the bag of money up, over and into the bin, making a mental note of where it landed in the pile. Fortunately the bin looked pretty empty. He wheeled back around to Simpson.

'Happy?'

But the boy was already walking away whistling to himself. Phil was watching him with the faintest hint of amusement. Aaron licked his moustache. As long as Phil was stood out here he couldn't come and get the money.

'You coming in or what?'

Phil nodded at his cigarette again.

'On break.'

***

The vicar was is a panic. Every year the egg hunt was a nightmare to organise. He knew that already. Everyone in the church knew that for crying out loud. That was why no one ever wanted to be involved. Oh yes, it's all well and good coming to church on a Sunday but as soon as you actually have to put a spot of effort in suddenly everyone becomes very busy. Very busy indeed.

Why oh why had he decided to give the responsibility to a couple of kids this year? What on earth had been thinking? Certainly, that young Simon boy had done a wonderful job with the graveyard. He could hardly fault the lad's character but he was in way over his depth. And that Maisie girl? Well, he'd given her a chance. Especially after she seemed to be growing into a proper young women. But really, this could hardly be good for his heart.

Where could they have possibly got to? He'd scoured the entire field twice over and seen neither hide nor hair of either of them. What's worse, the eggs were all missing! All one hundred of them, just gone. Now he was utterly powerless to anything other than flap.

Children would be arriving at any moment and – there they were! The vicar spotted Maisie's awful jumper disappearing around the back of Bella and Aled's car. Ignoring his slowly collapsing lungs he adopted what he hoped was a sufficiently stern expression and strode over in their direction. They were running their own stall which was fair enough but the egg hunt should come first. No, it *had* to come first.

'Excuse me. Maisie, excuse me!'

The girl poked her head out from behind the car and beamed at him. The vicar was so taken aback he almost toppled over there and then. In all his years, he'd never – never – received anything so much as a half-smile from the girl and now she was grinning at him as if butter wouldn't melt.

'Hey. How's it going?'

'It is um…. Well, quite frankly it is a shambles, my dear. Where on earth have the eggs gone?'

'Eggs?'

'The eggs that yourself and young Simon are supposed to have hidden already?'

'Oh right! Of course, yeah. They're right here. Don't you worry 'bout a thing.'

She beckoned him over behind the car and much to the vicar's astonishment young Simon was there too, sat humbly on a bin bag to stop the grass from wetting his behind with two distinct mountains of eggs in front of him. The boy gave him the exact same smile as Maisie. How on earth had he missed the pair of them sitting here on the grass? A couple of his marbles must have rolled away overnight.

'Morning.'

'Good morning, Simon. I hope that the eggs are ready to be hidden. The children will be arriving soon.'

'Yep, just doing the last checks on them. Got to make sure they're all there.'

The vicar nodded. Much to his surprised the pair of them seemed very much to be on top of everything. Most strange indeed.

'Right. Well, you will need to run and hide them soon. Just don't forget.'

'We won't.'

Simon beamed up at him again with a hint of concern.

'Are you feeling okay? You look exhausted.'

'Why yes, my boy. I'm feeling fine, thank you.'

But he quickly realised he wasn't. All of this flustering and flapping had quite taken the wind out of his sails. Maisie laid a hand on his shoulder.

'We've got it covered, don't you worry. Go have a sit down and a cuppa.'

'Right, yes. Yes. Thank you, the pair of you. It is appreciated, what you're doing.'

'It's no problem at all, now go and sit down. We'll sort the eggs.'

The vicar rested his hand in the boot of a car to catch his breath momentarily before making his departure. There was something smooth under his fingertips. As he ambled away he had to wonder why on earth Bella and Aled would need two pairs of high visibility jackets in the boot of their car.

***

Jonesy couldn't help but grin as all the kids were released out on their egg hunt. It wasn't a big primary school here. Of course it wasn't, this town was the middle of nowhere, but it was a good school. He could just about make out his daughter in the crowd, pigtails bouncing, pink jacket thrown to the floor as soon as she started running. She was dressed as a fairy after all, it would be a shame to wear a coat over that. He made a mental note where she'd left it as he watched the swarm of children disperse from the safety of his stall.

Most people were probably put off by the smell of fish wafting from his table. He never did very good business at the town fete. He'd put it down to people wanting to buy candy floss over cod and honestly he couldn't blame them all that much. Still, his catches recently had improved. Over the last week or so he'd noticed the crabs that he'd pick up from his boxes every morning had started getting bigger again. For a while they'd been a bit on the small side.

He supposed he couldn't really compete with all of the stalls around the place this year. There were all the usual crowd selling cakes, old toys, and books but there were a couple of new stalls too. A couple of young people were selling what looked like homemade jumpers. They looked warm, exactly the kind of thing he'd need in winter. He was just wondering whether to go up to the lad and lass when he spotted that weasel from the supermarket storming over to them. Best to leave it a bit he reckoned.

***

Aaron was a man who prided himself on a lot of things. Every morning he'd look in the mirror and see an attractive man. Too attractive for a place like this. He was also a good man. He ran the supermarket better than anybody else could. Every night he'd sit at his computer watching videos and reading articles about how to be a great leader. And he *was* one too. He was a great teacher, a great speaker, a funny man, a charming man, noble, selfless, strong, and humble.

But if there was one that Aaron was not, oh boy was he not, it was a coward. No siree. He was not afraid of anything, least of all Simpson and his little girlfriend. He would give them a piece of his mind, that's what he would do. Thinking they could just walk into his town and disrespect him like that? Well, they had another thing coming.

There he was minding his own business behind his desk, thinking all was right with the world. Well almost all. All of his savings – yes, that's what they were, savings, not dirty money at all, just a business expense – *all* of his savings were sat in the bins outside. But that was fine. You know why? No one else knew. The only people who'd seen him take the bag out were Simpson and Phil and both of them were too braindead to know shit.

That's right. He was fine. He had nothing to worry about at all. He just had to wait for Phil to finally haul his arse inside and then he could go out for some 'air', hop in the bin and get his savings back out. He'd figured it out. He'd hide them in the ceiling of his office. That was good. That way, if that brat did call the police on him all they'd find would be an empty safe. Well, almost empty.

He'd had the foresight to put a couple of pictures from his desk in there to throw them off. He'd even prepared lies about who they were pictures of. One was his dead grandma who'd told him to follow his dreams. The other was his dead dog who'd stayed with him when he'd broken his arm as a boy. Really they were both just stock photos that had come in the frames but the police didn't need to know that.

That was that, he'd wait for Phil to come in and then get the bag and then hide the money in the ceiling. He couldn't help but feel a little proud of himself. He'd have to add ingenuity to the list of things he prided himself on.

And there, right on the dot was the sound of Phil coming in. Aaron rubbed his hands together and got up from his desk. He went out into the shop where Charlotte and Phil were sat in their usual places. He cleared his throat and, with a line so well-rehearsed he doubted either of them could see through his rouse, announced he was going outside.

'Excuse me, but I need to go out and get some fresh air. It's a beautiful day after all. The thirteenth rule of business: nature. It's wonderful, use it to guide and inspire you.'

He'd improvised that last bit. He couldn't help but grin as he walked out of the front doors and ducked round the side of the building. The grin remained on his face all the way round to the back. It stayed there as he spotted the exact bin his savings were sat in. It was even there as he lifted the lid, forgetting about the flood of bin juice that splashed his other shoe. But when Aaron looked into the bin, his smile faltered and fell into a look of horror.

'Phil!'

Aaron didn't like to shout at his employees but desperate times called for such action.

'Phil, you fat oaf! Get the hell out here right now! PHIL!'

A muffled voice came from inside the shop.

'I'm on duty.'

'IF YOU DON'T GET OUT HERE THIS SECOND YOU'RE FIRED!'

There was a groan from inside, the door opened slowly and Phil stepped out, looking as bemused as ever.

'Where the hell is my – is *the* rubbish?'

Phil shrugged.

'Answer me!'

'Dunno.'

'What d'you mean dunno?!'

'Could be anywhere by now.'

'Who took it?'

'Who do you think?'

'I'M FUCKING ASKING YOU.'

'Bin men.'

'What fucking bin men?'

Phil shrugged.

'Dunno. Didn't ask their names.'

Aaron mouthed words noiselessly. Phil just stood there impatiently.

'I'm on duty. Need to be inside.'

'Go! Fucking fuck off!!'

Aaron was losing it. He could feel all control slipping away from him. The bin men? The bin men?! All that money he'd been saving for years just gone into the back of a truck. Wait, the truck. Phil was already in the doorway.

'Phil, wait! Where was the truck? I didn't see a truck.'

Phil shrugged again. He'd almost disappeared through the door when he stopped and popped his head back out.

'Didn't see no truck but one of them was a chick. Dunno, thought that was very progressive. Twenty first century and all. Guess that means I shouldn't be calling them bin men anymore.'

He looked slightly puzzled for a moment, then his face returned to its usual bemused state and he disappeared inside. Aaron stood there trembling with rage for a moment. Then he was off, heading straight for the field across the road.

***

'SIMPSON!'

A lot of the parents around Aaron gasped and pulled their costumed kids away instinctively. He was no coward, especially not to Simpson. No one would make a fool out of him. No one. Simpson was standing behind the stupid stall of his wearing a god awful knitted jumper. That girl was with him. They both turned to look at Aaron in unison.

'WHERE IS IT?'

More gasps. Aaron was roaring loud enough for the whole town to hear but he didn't care an ounce. Those two little shits had stolen his money. The girl answered him.

'Where's what?'

'Shut up, bitch.'

Simpson bristled.

'*Hey*. Don't you *dare* speak to her like that.'

She punched Simpson's arm.

'Hey, piss off. I can defend myself.'

She turned back to Aaron.

'What d'you want?'

'MY GODDAMN –'

But he stopped himself just in time. A lot of people were watching and listening. Suddenly, Aaron's courage faltered. His knees wobbled slightly. When he started speaking again his voice didn't sound as brave as he wanted.

'You know what I'm talking about.'

'Give us a clue.'

'You've fucking stolen it, how's that?'

They both gave him these innocent confused little faces as if they'd never done anything wrong in their damn lives. Well, that just wouldn't fly. He'd show them.

'Your costumes, where the hell are they?'

'Costumes?'

'You're bin men outfits – bin woman outfits – fucking bin people outfits, where are they? Got changed pretty quick did you?'

The two of them looked at each other confused. They were awful actors. They thought they were so smart, huh? Well he could see right through it. He'd get them, oh he'd get them alright. He was just about to start yelling again when a hand appeared on his shoulder. It was the vicar, the damn vicar!

'What the hell do you want?'

'This is a family event. There are children all around.'

'Ah, fuck the kids.'

The vicar looked like he was gonna have a heart attack there and then. Aaron grinned.

'Yeah, that's right. I don't give a shit. They can hear me swear as much as they want. They all do it anyway, look at 'em. Little fuckers!'

Someone cleared their throat behind him. Aaron whirled round ready to keep shouting and stopped immediately. His face dropped.

'Officer.'

'Do we have a problem here, Aaron?'

'No, sir. No problem at all.'

'Are you sure about that,? Never that good at keeping your cool back in highschool, were you?'

'I'm better now.'

'Sure about that? What's all this disturbance about?'

Simpson jumped in before Aaron could figure out an answer.

'He says we've stolen something from him.'

'Oh really? And what have they stolen Aaron?'

Aaron mouthed wordlessly again. That damn kid. He'd get him. Oh, he'd get him.

'Simpson, you little...'

'My name's Simon. I've been here the whole time, when would I have stolen anything?'

'That's not true!'

The vicar stepped in, addressing the officer.

'It is true. I can vouch for him.'

The officer turned to Aaron eyebrows raised. Aaron had no choice. He shut his mouth, turned around and stalked off. He'd get them, oh he'd get them. The money was hiding somewhere and he'd sure as hell find it.

Just at that moment, he spotted a pile of bin bags behind a gazebo. He'd never been so happy to see a rubbish heap in all his life.

***

Penny was always late down to the fete. It was her knees really. They weren't agreeing with downhills quite as well as they used to. In fact, she was wondering quite what effect the walk had had on her as she rounded the end of the school and spied a skinny weasel of a man headfirst in a pile of bin bags. She paused to watch him. He ripped one open, poured the contents all over the grass, sifted around through the plastics, old foods, and what-have-you, punched the ground and moved on to the next. It was most peculiar indeed.

He caught her watching him and looked at her like a rabbit in the headlights. Then he raised a tentative hand in her direction. After a moment she found herself giving him a little wave in return. He wasn't bad looking, that lad. He had a rather fetching little moustache on him. A shy smile curled it up at the corners.

***

Five eggs! Five whole eggs. One, two, three, four, five. Last year she only got two. Now she had five, five eggs! She ran up to show daddy every single one of them. He looked very happy. His fish were smelly and his crabs were yucky so she ran away again. Five whole eggs! Five! Oh boy.

What was that silly man doing in the rubbish? There weren't any eggs in there. Silly man.

Five!

***

Bella couldn't help but smiling at she watched Simon running his little stall. She had to admit, she was quite impressed with him. With the pair of them really. Aled caught her staring and nudged her with a little smile on his face.

'Oh Aled, they've done well haven't they?'

'Mhm.'

'I mean, those jumpers. They're nice. Actually nice. And the one she's knitted for him. Oh it's gorgeous Aled. Reminds me of Huw's one. Who knew she had it in her?'

Aled grunted.

'Okay, fine. Maybe you knew.'

Bella watched them a moment longer. Simon was smiling again. Properly smiling. Not that pretend smile he gave her all the time. And Maisie. Well, she was just Maisie wasn't she? But maybe that wasn't such a bad thing.

'You know Aled…'

But the words didn't come. He put his arm around her and gave her that little squeeze that always made her chest flutter a little bit, even after all these years.

'I know.'

***

And so the day went by as it would every other year. Aunt Bella sold her fruitcakes. Uncle Aled sold fish. Jonesy tried to sell crabs. The children found egg after egg. Simon and Maisie sold jumpers; a lot of jumpers. The one exception to all that was going on was Aaron, who thundered around the place searching high and low. But everyone just thought he was just taking part in the egg hunt. And of course, the vicar was flapping again.

'Simon, my boy. Simon.'

'You okay? You're looking a bit-'

'My boy, the egg hunt ends in just fifteen minutes!'

'Okay, cool.'

'Are you ready?'

'Yeah, of course.'

'No but you don't understand. The children, they…'

'I think we can handle a few kids.'

'But the prizes, my boy!'

'We've got the prizes sorted, don't worry.'

Maisie was giggling slightly but refolded a couple of jumpers so the vicar wouldn't notice. His hearing was deteriorating after all.

'Simon, my boy. I very much appreciate your calmness here but I'm afraid that I cannot share in it.'

'That's fine, just go and have a sit down. Maisie and I will collect all the eggs in and give out prizes.'

'Right yes. A sit down.'

'That's what you need right now.'

'A sit down. Why yes, indeed.'

Simon watched the vicar walk off with a faint smile on his face but it soon faded. He turned to Maisie who didn't look much different to how he felt. She was picking at her sleeve under the table. He followed her vision and soon picked out Aaron stalking this way and that between stalls, eyes darting this way and that.

'Ready, Maisie?'

'This is the tricky bit.'

'This is the tricky bit.'

The elderly couple that had spoken to Simon outside church came by and bought a pair of jumpers. Simon and Maisie smiled easily at them but again their smiles faded as soon as they were no longer being watched.

***

Aaron spotted his opportunity and leapt on it. Simpson and that girl had got up and left their stupid jumper stall unattended. Idiots. He'd show them, oh how he'd show them. With a brilliant piece of acting on his part, Aaron started to whistle, stuck his hands in his pockets and strolled over to their stall. No one paid him any attention. Oh, he'd get them alright.

Their stall was awful. A bunch of ugly homemade looking jumpers that a five year old could've done. Aaron knocked one onto the floor pretending it was an accident. He didn't pick it up. He glanced around nonchalantly to check the coast was clear before diving round behind the stall and ducking under the table. Man, he was pretty good at this. He'd watched a lot of movies; that was probably why.

There were bags under the table. Plenty of bags. Aaron grinned and started sifting through them. His would be there, he knew it. God, they were stupid just leaving all his money here like that. Well, he did suppose they were dealing with *him* after all. Not just anyone. No siree, it would take a lot more brains than that to steal from him. Oh, he'd show them.

The first bag had nothing in it at all. The next one, just a few scraps of paper and a half-used roll of masking tape. Aaron clenched the tape in his hand for a moment. He'd kind of hoped to bend it out of shape but he couldn't quite manage it so he threw it behind him instead.

'Hello?'

Aaron froze. It sounded like a little girl. He'd have to be quick. He ripped open the next bag but it just had jumpers in it. He threw jumper after jumper behind him but that's all there were. Jumpers. One last bag. He was just reaching for it when a pair of legs appeared next to the table. There was some fabric just about hiding him from view, until a pair of eyes appeared in the gap at the bottom.

'Hello mister.'

'Um, what's up?'

'I've got five eggs!'

The girl's pigtails brushed the grass. She beamed at him. Aaron gave what he hoped was a convincing smile back.

'That's nice.'

'Are you hiding?'

'No. I, uh, I'm seeking.'

The little girl furrowed her eyebrows.

'There's no eggs in there.'

Then a mischievous grin appeared on her lips.

'I already checked.'

'You didn't see anything else down here did ya?'

'Jumpers. Rubbish. Feet.'

'Any... any money?'

The little girl thought hard for a moment then shook her head, pigtails swinging.

'No, mister.'

Aaron's head hit his hands. He felt a little hand on his shoulder.

'Don't cry mister. I lose things all the time. Then daddy finds them.'

The hand pulled away quickly. Aaron looked up to see the girl looking very concerned.

'Y'alright?'

'My coat!'

And the little girl ran off leaving Aaron on his own under the table. He ripped the last bag open out of ceremony and had all but given up when he heard that Maisie girl shouting something nearby.

'Time's up for the egg hunt! Bring your eggs over here and we'll count 'em up for you!'

Aaron sat there under the table for a long time thinking. He could hear dozens of little footsteps rushing past him all carrying little baskets of eggs with little smiles on their faces. If he only he could just go around collecting eggs and be happy with it. He'd probably have more luck. A jolt ran through his body. He was up and out from under the table tripping and tumbling over the bags as he went.

'SIMPSON!'

Half of the kids in the little swarm jumped and turned to him frightened. If they were scared now, he'd show them something really scary in a second.

'SIMPSON!'

Simpson rose out of the crowd of kids. Aaron couldn't help noticing how tall the boy was. Who cared though? He was no coward.

'Can I help you?'

'Can you help me? Can *you* help *me*?'

'What is it this time?'

Aaron had the eyes of the whole town on him now. His knees wobbled a bit but he stayed up and cleared his throat. If he had everyone's attention then so be it. He didn't even care that the police were there anymore. He would get his money and he would show that boy. Oh he'd show him.

'Well, if everyone wants to hear this then fine. This boy right here is a thief. Nothing but a no good lying little thief.'

'Oh, this again.'

'Yeah, this again. You might be fooling them but you can't fool me, Simpson.'

'Simon.'

'SHUT UP.'

The few murmurs that had been floating around stopped. Aaron took a deep breath and tried to compose himself.

'You think you're so clever, don't you? Well guess what, I'm more clever.'

'Cleverer.'

'Yeah? Let's see how cleverer you are then, huh?'

Aaron snatched an egg out the nearest basket. It was the girl with the pigtails. She shouted at him indignantly but he ignored it.

'Watch! Everybody watch. This *boy* thinks he's so smart that he can steal from me.'

'Aaron, please stop.'

But Aaron could see something in Simpson's eye. The corner was twitching slightly. At that moment, the girl appeared from out behind that car they'd arrived in. He could see her fiddling with her sleeve. He'd gott them. Oh, he'd got them!

'You wanna tell them all what's in the egg Simpson? Or should I?'

'I don't know what you're on about.'

'Oh you do. I've got you now boy.'

Aaron held the egg high over his head and pulled the two halves apart. In that moment he reckoned he knew how Jesus felt when he broke that bread of whatever with everyone watching. They were all wide-eyed and open mouthed. He grinned triumphantly but they all just stared back at him.

Aaron looked up at the two halves of the egg. It was empty. Completely empty. No, that couldn't be right. He threw the halves on the ground and snatched the next egg out of the girl's basket. This time she kicked him in the shin, hard. It took all his self-control not to kick her back. Hopping on one leg he pulled apart the next egg but again nothing.

'Aaron.'

'Shut up!'

'Aaron!'

'SHUT UP! YOU'VE GOT MY MONEY, WHERE IS IT?!'

Aaron charged at Simpson. The sea of kids had parted leaving just the two of them facing each other. At the last second Simpson sidestepped him, leaving Aaron to fly sprawling onto the grass. He only just missed hitting his head on the car. The car!

He scrambled to his feet and ran round the back of the car. The boot lid was open. High visibility jackets! He snatched one up and waved it above his head.

'The bin people! The bin people!'

The whole town looked nonplussed. He threw the jacket on the floor and started digging through the boot. Nothing. Nothing! He grabbed at the corner of the upholstery and gave it a tug. There was a ripping sound. Aaron cried triumphantly just as a pair of big hands grabbed him and threw him onto his back.

The four of them were standing over him. Simpson, his girlfriend, and those two old people who looked after them. Aaron spat on the grass tried to get up. The man unfolded his arms and that was all it took to keep Aaron down.

'Those kids, those *brat kids*. Fucking thieves! I'll get you, oh god how I'll get you.'

The old lady stepped forwards.

'They're not thieves. Simon is my nephew and Maisie is… Maisie is a *fine* young woman.'

The other three looked as surprised as Aaron felt but the lady, the aunt, kept going.

'If you harass these two again, I will not hesitate to call the police. You understand? This is *my* family and you will not touch a hair on their heads. Do you understand?'

Simpson grinned. Maisie was looking at the floor all red faced. The uncle was still towering over him, sleeves rolled up. He had no choice. Maybe he'd get them one day but for now he only had one option. Aaron rolled over, scrambled up to his feet and ran.

***

Jonesy couldn't help smiling as he watched that weasel run home. The smile remained on his face all afternoon, long after he'd forgotten all about that man, because his little girl came back to him beaming with joy. All she had to show for her prize from the egg hunt were a couple of chocolate bars and a packet of Haribos but she was grinning from ear to ear all afternoon.

'Five eggs. Five!'

Just as everyone was packing away under the warm pink sky, he wandered over to the jumper stall. The lad running it was called Simon, he couldn't quite place where he'd seen him before but they'd definitely spoken. He was sure of that. The lad was very decent, gave him a heavy discount on a nice thick winter jumper. The girl disappeared while they were chatting, whispering something to Simon as she went. He chatted to the lad for a while longer before going to pack away.

Anyway, it hadn't been a great day selling. Only a few crabs and a couple fish. Not really worth the trip out here honestly. He should have just come as a dad to spend the day with his little girl. But as he lifted the last crab to put back into the ice he noticed something masking taped to its leg. His eyes must have been playing tricks again. If he didn't know better he'd have thought it was a roll of cash.

***

For the first time that day, the vicar finally had a chance to catch his breath. Most of the stands were gone. The field was looking larger and larger with every gazebo, table, and car that disappeared. He supposed the egg hunt had indeed been somewhat of a success. He watched young Simon and that Maisie girl as they packed the last of their jumpers into the back of the car. They gave him a wave as they hopped into the backseat. The tail lights were on as they drove out.

It was getting late. With a mighty sigh the vicar stood up from his camping chair and folded it up. An envelope fell to the floor. He must have been sitting on it. It took him a while to bend all the way down to retrieve it. It was addressed to him. He ran his finger along the top, ripping the paper open. When he saw what was inside he immediately put the chair back down and fell into it. Nestled in between all the money was a little handwritten note.

For the repairs and maintenance of the graveyard.

***

Aaron didn't stop walking all day. He walked back to the supermarket, all the way around it, then out again onto the streets where he walked well into the night. He'd been licking his moustache constantly. His top lip was raw. He found himself on the other end of the coastal path in the small little neighbouring town. There was that awful little church and, beyond it, a pub.

Aaron licked his moustache and made a beeline for the door. The place was nearly empty. A clock on the wall told him it wasn't today anymore. It was tomorrow now. He threw himself down on a stool at the bar and shouted for shots. He didn't much care who brought them, what they were, or how many he had.

Three little tiny glasses appeared in his vision and he necked one after the other and called for more straight away. He wretched but managed to keep it in. He hadn't eaten since breakfast, there'd be nothing to come up anyway. After a little while staring at the table, two more appeared and he slammed them.

A pair of hands grabbed him from behind. Aaron swung around to punch but missed entirely. A large man filled his vision. His focus was already starting to dip in and out. When the large man spoke it was in a thick slurred accent.

'You wanna be careful mate.'

Aaron tried to shrug the arms off with no luck.

'Drinking all them shots so quick... can't be good.'

'Piss off.'

'Ay, ya better watch it with me. What's got your knickers in a twist, eh?'

Aaron wrenched himself free and turned back to the bar. Then all of a sudden he spun back around.

'This little bitch stole from me. She and her boyfriend bled me dry, dry! I'm done. I'm broke. Fourteen thousand pounds. Fourteen. Thousand.'

The man ran a hand through the tied up mop of hair on his head, a look of genuine surprise on his face. Finally something interesting was happening in this town.

'Say, what's this girl's name?'

'I don't know, like Maisie or something. Stupid brat who wears ugly jumpers, fucking annoying voice and all.'

Maisie's dad knocked Aaron out with his first punch.

***

The sea slept quietly, foamy white head resting on the rocks.

There wasn't a boat in sight to disturb its peace.

Chapter 15

The sun was too bright. Simon couldn't see his phone screen properly. He tried to shield it from the light but even then he had to squint to make anything out. He only had one bar of signal and it was dipping in and out. This one patch of cliff was the one place he'd managed to find where he could get any reception.

The wind tugged at his shirt but he ignored it. He'd lost track of how long he'd been away from home. At first he'd been so good at counting the days and weeks but something had made him forget about all of that. It couldn't have been too long though. Definitely not long enough for everything to have changed so much. He barely recognised the people in the photos he was scrolling through. The wind tugged at his shirt again and this time Simon glanced up. Maisie was watching him from a few feet away.

'Nice phone.'

'God, don't sneak up on me like that.'

'Mate, I coulda been playing the trumpet and you still wouldn't look up from that thing.'

'Sorry.'

Simon locked the phone and slid it back into his pocket. It felt good having a full pocket again. The phone felt big. Noticeable.

'Space on the rock for one more?'

'Yeah sure.'

Simon shuffled over. The rock was warm to touch. Looking around he noticed it was actually quite a nice day. The sun was just about peeking out from behind the clouds. Large shadows floated lazily across the sea. A warm breeze was dancing around. Maisie plonked herself down next to Simon and immediately started chattering away.

'So I was thinking about my jumpers, right? Basically, I kind of want them all to have this uniform look but like not properly uniform because they all need to be different but they should all have something that makes people look at them and be like "That's a Maisie jumper" you know? And I'm just trying to figure out what that *thing* would be. Do I wanna start putting a logo on them? Or do I have a colour pallet for them? But then I can't have a colour pallet because your jumper doesn't fit with anything else I've made.'

Simon just sat back on the rock and listened to her talk at him. Since they'd pulled off their heist Maisie had been living on cloud nine, talking non-stop about her dreams for the future and exactly how she was going to start working on them. He supposed she probably had to keep her mind off the other stuff that had been happening.

Her dad had been arrested the night of the town fete. Simon heard about it the next day from a dog walker up on the path. Apparently, Aaron had gone to the pub that night and started mouthing off about Maisie in front of her dad. The police were called in. Simon half-remembered being woken up by the sirens.

From what Maisie had said the charges all mounted up pretty quickly. The police had found some weed on him and gone to search the caravan, which was already illegal itself. On top of that, there were more drugs inside, papers pointing to some shady business dealings, and he himself admitted to a slew of other things.

Simon had expected Maisie to be upset about it but when he finally had asked her about it all she'd smiled. Apparently, she'd gone to visit her dad and they'd spent a long time talking, properly talking, about everything. She didn't tell Simon quite what they'd said. He didn't want to push her for any details she didn't want to share. All he knew was that her dad had apparently seemed like himself for the first time in a long time. He reckoned when you have that many demons following you around it must be a something to face them all at once like that.

Aaron, on the other hand, hadn't fared so well from it all. It was probably for the best that the first punch had knocked him out because all of the follow up ones had done the real damage. He was being treated in a hospital out of town, about an hour's drive up the coast. Uncle Aled had been quite surprised at Simon's request to drive him but agreed nonetheless. His uncle waited in the car.

Simon had been pretty hesitant to approach the bed. Aaron's face was covered in bandages so Simon wasn't even sure he was by the right bed until that familiar voice, slightly softer than usual, came through the gauze.

'The hell d'you want? Come to laugh at me?'

'No.'

'Just piss off, Simpson. You've done enough, alright?'

'I'm here to say sorry.'

'Yeah well I don't want it, alright? Just leave me alone. I hate you and I hate that ugly bitch girlfriend of yours.'

Looking down at Aaron, covered in bandages, trying not to wince every time he moved. Simon couldn't feel angry at him. He placed the bag he'd brought with him on the bedside. There was a bouquet of flowers there with a note signed *P xx*. He trying to touch Aaron on the shoulder but the man wriggled away. The doctors had had to shave his moustache away to deal with his busted lip.

'Aaron, I know it's not enough. You don't deserve any of this. Um, yeah. I don't know. I'm sorry. Just, I hope you get better. That supermarket won't run itself.'

He turned to leave. He was almost out of the door when Aaron called out to him.

'Who made this?'

Simon turned back to see Aaron had taken the jumper out of the bag and was holding it up. On it Maisie had embroidered Aaron's face on Luke Skywalker as he trained in the swamp. Simon smiled slightly.

'My ugly bitch girlfriend.'

Aaron tried not to smile back but couldn't hide it when he looked back at the jumper. Simon watched him from the doorway.

'And for the record, I think you look a lot better without the moustache.'

''At's probably because the bandages are covering up the rest of me.'

'Take care of yourself, Aaron.'

'Simon.'

Aaron was due to come out of hospital in the next few days. None of his injuries had been too bad, the doctors mainly were just keeping him in to be sure that his head was okay. The concussion can't have been nice.

Aside from his absence in the supermarket, the rest of the town was exactly as it always had been. Just with a few little differences. He'd started to play the Casio at church on Sundays with Maisie singing. They were trying to introduce a couple of new songs. That was pretty good.

Oh and Maisie came round for dinner virtually every night now. She'd sheepishly offered Huw's wallet to Aunt Bella but that had been shot down almost instantly. If Huw gave her the wallet then it was hers, end of. As soon as that conversation had been had, it was as if a spell had broken over the house. The pictures on the walls smiled properly again.

Sometimes in the evening, once he was sure everyone was asleep, Simon would grab the shoe box out from under his bed. Quietly as he could, he'd tip the neatly rolled money onto the duvet and look at it for a while. He mostly did it because he felt like he was supposed to but honestly it didn't really do anything for him. He'd inevitably shove it all back into the box again and lie back thinking about... well, thinking about stuff.

He still had no idea quite how they'd pulled it off. Some good planning from him and Maisie only went so far. Something - or someone - else entirely had carried them through. They'd staged the conversation about calling the police on Aaron as soon as they saw he was within earshot. He really wasn't good at hiding at all and they'd had a good laugh about it since.

The first stroke of luck had come from Aaron hiding the money in the bins. They'd had a couple of contingency plans for different hiding spots but the bins out back had always been their plan A. They'd only just managed to stash the money in the eggs when the vicar had popped up. Maisie had been right about how risky it was to tape the money to the insides of the eggs. They'd managed to go the whole day without Aaron realising until right at the last minute.

Honestly, they still had no clue how they got away with that. They weren't entirely sure why the eggs that he'd grabbed off that little girl were empty but their final total *had* come up short. About five eggs short. Simon smiled to himself.

Maisie stopped talking and was looking at him.

'You weren't listening to any of that were you?'

'Sure, I was.'

'Alright, then dickhead. What was I chatting about?'

'Jumpers.'

'Mhm. And?'

'Err...'

'God, you're lucky I like you, you know that?'

Simon grinned at her. She rolled her eyes but couldn't help smiling back. He touched her arm.

'Maisie, we did it. We actually did it.'

She laughed. He'd been saying that to her constantly for the past few days.

'Yeah, I know. I was there genius.'

'How was the flat you looked at?'

'Pretty basic but you know what they say. Home is home, no matter how poor it is. Besides, it's right by the sea.'

'So it'll fall in in a couple of years?'

'Ah, I'll be jetting off to Milan long before that happens.'

'Speaking of jetting off...'

The breeze died down. Maisie's smile faltered. Simon pressed on anyway. He needed to say it.

'I've booked my train back to London.'

Maisie didn't reply.

'It leaves tomorrow night.'

Silence.

'I got first class as well, figured I could afford to splash out a bit.'

'Tomorrow?'

'Yeah.'

'Are you serious?'

'Yup. By tomorrow night I'll be back where I belong, might get a house in Kensington. You reckon they accept cash?'

'Stop talking.'

Maisie got up from the rock they were sitting on and walked to the edge of the cliff. The wind returned. Softly at first, then Simon started to hear a distance howl.

'You're actually going back to London?'

'Well, yeah. I rang mum yesterday. Told her I bought a new phone and learned my lesson and she said she'd start making my bed.'

'Fuck you.'

'Maisie?'

'Shut up. Alright? Just shut up and tell me you're joking.'

'I'm confused, do you want me to talk or not?'

'*Simon.*'

'I'm not joking. I'm sorry but I'm going home. We can still keep in contact. We *will* still keep in contact. I'll come and visit like all the time.'

'I can't believe you.'

Maisie turned back to him. There were tears in her eyes.

'Maisie, what's wrong?'

'Oh, shut up.'

'Look, I don't want to leave either, okay? But I have a life back home.'

'And you don't have a life here?'

'Maisie, come on. Don't make this difficult.'

'*I'm* making this difficult? *Me*?'

'What's this all about?'

'Oh, don't even start.'

The wind was really blowing now. It tore Maisie's hair this way and that. Simon stood up and closed the gap between them.

'I'm serious, what's wrong?'

'You're actually gonna make me say it, aren't you?'

'Say what?'

'Oh, come on!'

'What is it Maisie?'

'I d'know. I've just been sat here with my big dumb imagination thinking maybe you'd come here and tell me that you like me. And then I'd laugh at you and call you a loser. Then you'd walk away all upset... and, I don't know, maybe I'd run up and kiss you or something stupid. And you could say all the soppy shit because I'm not good at it. And you could stay here and not go back to London. And we could get a place together and actually, you know, be a couple or something and this is all dumb and you're dumb and *I'm* dumb for thinking all this and I'm just waiting for you to tell me to shut up so I can stop embarrassing myself.'

'Maisie.'

'Actually, you know what? *You* shut up. I ain't done. Since this is the last time I'll see you I'm just gonna say it all. I hate your clothes, you dress like a rich twat. The only time you ever looked half-decent is in that jumper I made you. And guess what, that jumper took a month to make. I threw away four because they weren't good enough. And I hate your accent, your sound like a preppy little dickhead from Downton Abbey. And you've got a unibrow coming through. Your eyes are wonky. And stop being so likeable. You're supposed to be arguing with me. You're making *me* look like the dickhead here. Well, you know what? It's fine. You've always been better than me anyway. Every time someone in town sees us together they look disappointed because their favourite little poster boy, that lovely lad from church, is hanging out with *Maisie*. What's he doing with *her*?'

'Maisie.'

'*What?* What are you gonna say? You're cancelling your tickets to London? Yeah, right.'

'Maisie, I... I'm sorry.'

'Oh brilliant. Thanks for that. I'm glad you've got that off your chest. Must've been real hard to say.'

Her voice cracked on the last word. Simon could see her trying to regain control. She was losing. The wind buffeted them so hard it threatened to knock them both off balance. Simon opened his mouth and closed it again. He could feel something in his chest breaking.

'Maisie.'

'No. Alright, no more. I'm done.'

'Let's talk about this.'

'Bit fucking late for that. Enjoy your new phone, hope it makes you happy.'

A passerby watched as the girl stormed off down the path leaving that lovely lad from church stood up on the cliff all on his own. The boy stayed there in that same spot for a long time, as the wind died around him.

***

The car journey to Cardiff was a quiet one. Simon stared out of the window as those cliffs he'd gotten so used to flattened into motorways, then rose into houses, towns, and cities. The sky was identical to how it had been when he'd first arrived in Wales; grey and flat.

Aunt Bella had been wearing a smile all day but it slipped as they got closer and closer to the station. Uncle Aled didn't say a word. There wasn't really much to say. Simon was going home and that was that. It was going to happen eventually. And eventually had just arrived. Aunt Bella half-heartedly suggested they stop off and get a bite to eat but she knew they couldn't. Simon had a train to catch at 17:08 on the dot. They were out of time.

A car beeped somewhere behind them.

***

Maisie was stupid. At least now she knew she was. It had been dumb to come back up here. That rock wasn't anymore special than any other rock out here. Of course he hadn't come back. He was gone and that was that.

She sat down on the rock anyway and put the walkie-talkie next to her.

It didn't crackle.

The jumper hung still on the fencepost.

***

Simon dumped his suitcase on the rack and settled himself in his chair. His phone buzzed.

He glanced out of the window one last time before checking it. Aunt Bella and Uncle Aled were probably in the car going home already. Definitely too late to change his mind. Not that he wanted to.

He pulled the phone out of his pocket and unlocked it.

His mum had sent him a picture.

It was his bed at home freshly made.

The time ticked over to 17:08.

There were a new set of sheets on his bed.

***

The girl sat on that rock as the world moved around her. The sun set. The stars appeared.

The walkie-talkie sat with her.

She started shivering.

A little tune that she used to know as a kid came back to her.

In a tiny little voice she sang it to herself, looking at the sea.

The wind whistled the soft tune back to her.

Behind her, the boy leaned on his suitcase, listening.

He was trying to find the words that his aunt struggled with all those weeks ago on the beach.

She was…

She was Maisie.

And that was good enough.

A gust of wind caught the jumper hanging from the fencepost and carried it into the air.

Printed in Great Britain
by Amazon